SHADOW'S SIEGE

SHADOW ISLAND SERIES: BOOK FIFTEEN

MARY STONE
LORI RHODES

D1715419

MARY
STONE
PUBLISHING

This book is dedicated to the memory of Sheriff Deputy Greg McCowan, whose death hit way too close to home. Thank you for your service and your sacrifice. May you rest in peace, knowing you did your best to keep us all safe.

DESCRIPTION

Shadow Island is under siege.

Just a few short months ago, Sheriff Rebecca West thought her toughest battles were behind her. But nothing could have prepared her for the turmoil she's faced since coming to Shadow Island. Attempts on her life. Heartbreak. Betrayal. And that's just the beginning.

The worst is yet to come.

Still reeling from the shocking discovery of who's behind Shadow Island's exclusive and depraved "men's" club, Rebecca is determined to take them down. There's only one problem. One by one, the members end up dead. Tongues cut out, hands chopped off—the message is clear...

Dead witnesses can't talk. Now everyone is a potential victim.

Is there a traitor in the club's midst? An accomplice turned executioner? Or is the Yacht Club killing its own members rather than risking the police questioning them?

As the desperation of the masterminds behind the Yacht Club increases, so does the body count. In her relentless pursuit of the truth, Rebecca risks unraveling not just the secrets of the Yacht Club, but the very fabric of her own heart.

Shadow's Siege, the tensely climactic fifteenth installment of the Shadow Island Series by Mary Stone and Lori Rhodes, is a chilling reminder that just when you think things can't get worse, they do.

1

Attorney Braden Moore stood in his elegant, recently remodeled Spring Street office, rethinking his life choices. He'd never been able to tell his mom *no*, which should have been a good thing. Living like that should've made him a good person, a good son.

But did it? Of course not.

His mom was a degenerate gambler, and the relentless pressure to cover his mother's gambling debts had pushed him into the arms of a small-town law firm, a move that seemed rational at the time. The firm, owned by Steven Campbell, a former classmate from law school, had appeared to be Braden's lifeline—a chance to settle the debts and move forward.

Yet, as he watched his printer spew out page after page, he couldn't shake the feeling that this 'lifeline' was more of a noose. Joining Campbell's firm had thrust him into the murky waters of legal and moral ambiguity, far from the noble career he'd envisioned.

Making partner at an established firm before he was forty was a feat that impressed his year mates. They didn't know that Campbell had done shady business with his clients or that his dealings got him killed only one month after Braden had started, leaving him the sole owner of the firm.

While cleaning out Campbell's files, Braden had come across a bunch of familiar names. People who'd acted as witnesses, offered alibis, or posted bonds for Steven's clients. That was when he started piecing things together. Albert Gilroy's shady dealings, the work the firm did for the Yacht Club...these were damning details, hiding in plain sight in Campbell's papers.

Unknowingly, Braden had agreed to work for a criminal organization—and now he knew way more than any criminal defense attorney should've ever known about their clients and their client's associates.

When his phone started ringing around two that morning, he knew without checking what it meant. Another one of the Yacht Club goons had gotten into trouble, and they were expecting him to fix the problem.

After recognizing the caller, he'd listened to the rain pattering against the window, fearing it was the sound of someone breaking in and coming for him. This went on for hours as he tossed and turned. Sleep never returned, but he'd hatched a plan that he didn't know if he'd have the guts to follow through on—though as it turned out, he did.

He'd been ignoring their calls for ten hours now.

Refusing to help when they called was a death sentence. Although he'd been formulating a plan since Campbell had been gunned down, the clock didn't start officially ticking until the first call. He was getting the hell out of Dodge.

At the moment, his mom didn't owe anyone, and she swore she was in a twelve-step program to kick her addiction. That only ever lasted until the next sporting event, though.

Sighing, he knelt by the printer to reload it with paper. As soon as he closed the cover, it immediately began to whir again. He plucked up each document as it emerged.

With the rapid uptick in clients who'd been coming through his door and calling him at all hours over the past weeks, the Yacht Club seemed to be sinking fast. Considering how many of his clients had "accidents" in jail afterward, Braden didn't want to go down with the ship.

Attorney-client privilege only extended to facts shared between a client and their lawyer. Nothing Braden had incidentally overheard during Albert Gilroy's temper tantrums was covered. He'd confirmed this technicality with a friend who had nothing to do with the sordid business on Shadow Island.

Braden cursed the thin walls of the office he'd briefly shared with Campbell. Thanks to lousy insulation and cheap materials, he'd learned information never meant for him. And now he stood in front of the printer playing "catch the evidence."

He pulled files from a filing cabinet to add to the fresh stack of documents he'd printed. His perfectly tailored suit contrasted with his unkempt hair, and the dark circles under his eyes betrayed his inner turmoil.

So what if I look like hell? I'm taking my freedom.

Since first getting accepted into law school, his life had been a constant struggle between codependently helping his mother with her debts and practicing the kind of law he'd always dreamed about. Ultimately, he'd chosen his mother, a decision that now had him running for his life.

He turned to his desk. On the edge of the polished cherrywood surface sat a box filled with bulging folders. The first part of his plan was put together—it was his paycheck off the island and his shot to get his mom into a real recovery program instead of an amateur group run by volunteers in a church basement.

Each folder was filled with meticulous documentation he'd been compiling for the last few weeks. He knew the names of the people involved in the Yacht Club. It had taken just a little bit of digging to learn even more. At first, it had only been for his own morbid curiosity.

The thing about the low-level criminals he usually represented was they loved to talk. They especially enjoyed talking about their bosses. And once they thought their lawyer couldn't share that information, they blathered on and on about the good, the bad, and the ugly.

Braden hadn't explained to them the finer details of attorney-client privilege. For instance, crimes committed by other people weren't covered, especially if those crimes were part of an ongoing criminal act. Like Oswald Chapman's loan sharking. Or the blackmail schemes run by several other members.

The media was keyed into many of the names in his burgeoning files. And they'd pay top dollar for information exposing the powerful and prestigious elitists as nothing more than perverts and criminals.

Shining a spotlight on the breadth and depth of criminal activity on Shadow Island would serve multiple purposes. Braden would take down the Yacht Club so no one would be left to retaliate. He'd start his new life without looking over his shoulder. And he'd bank some real money to help his mother with an addiction she was unable to kick.

His hand lingered on an exceptionally large file. Only recently had he been able to connect the dots of a myriad of crimes all the way back to Jim and Vera Sawyer. His tired eyes scanned the pages. The Sawyers had put a hell of a lot of effort into concealing their positions within the criminal organization. Everyone in the club had participated in obscuring their involvement. But he'd been able to pull back the curtain and get a glimpse into their true selves.

They owned three homes, but only one was in their name. Their other assets were buried deeply within shell companies or offshore accounts. Their blue-collar son wasn't as he'd appeared either.

But I found them. And after I sell this information to the media, I'll make a fortune. Hell, I could probably get a book deal out of it.

And with the sordid details in these files, local jurisdictions and the Feds could begin to bring closure to the countless victims and their families. What he was doing was reckless, but so much good would come from his actions. And he'd be free to start over as a reputable lawyer.

Braden's hands trembled as he sorted through the files. His knowledge of the Sawyers' secret made him a target, and it sent shivers down his spine. Although he'd never personally met any of the Sawyers, the threat they posed was real.

But if I haven't dealt with them, I shouldn't even be on their radar. Maybe I'm freaking out over nothing.

None of Braden's clients lived on Shadow Island, since they were low-level members of the organization. And he made sure to keep their names out of the files he'd assembled. He was paid a retainer by a shell company that contacted him when they needed representation. Then he showed up and defended them. That was all he did. Jim and Vera Sawyer probably didn't even know who he was.

That was something he was thankful for. He was a nobody who neglected to answer a phone call. It was trivial.

Still, though. That one small act of defiance might draw attention. Getting noticed by "the bosses" led to a short life and painful death. That was common knowledge among his clients, even the more hardened ones.

He'd been regaled with stories, passed down through the ranks, of what the Sawyers did to anyone who disappointed or crossed them.

I could move my practice to Richmond and never look back.

For half a year, he'd taken care of these Yacht Club idiots. They talked to him like he wasn't even human, put on Earth to serve them. It would feel poetic to end up on top while everyone else burned.

Braden straightened his suit jacket and adjusted his tie, preparing to leave for his appointment with an editor from the *Daily Press*. The journalist had practically drooled over the phone at the idea of digging up dirt on Albert Gilroy. After running a front-page article about the man after his death, this would be the perfect "follow-up" piece.

The rain had let up, so he wouldn't need to struggle with an umbrella to protect the documents, but the box was heavy, and he only had two arms.

Once again, he wished he'd hired an intern or a receptionist who could open doors and run errands. Campbell had been adamant about not employing anyone else in the office, though. And since his partner had been gunned down in the street right outside their building, Braden hadn't been able to find anyone willing to work for him.

Eyeing the heavy box, he decided to open the door before worrying about schlepping the documents. He was reaching for the handle when the door swung outward, revealing a hulking figure whose broad shoulders blocked his path.

Braden's blood ran cold, his hand instinctively pulling back. Fear laced his every word as he stammered them out. "Who are you? What do you want?"

After an entire career of working with criminals, he'd learned to spot the difference between braggarts, two-bit thugs, and the ones who were truly dangerous. The hulk of a man staring at him definitely fell into that third category.

"I'm sorry, I'm just leaving to meet a client. You'll have to come back at another time. Let me check my calendar."

Words had always been Braden's best defense, and he deployed them to his advantage as he backed around his desk to put some distance between them.

The stranger's eyes glinted with menace as he closed the door, his movements deliberate and slow. "Sit down." His voice was low and gravelly.

Braden's legs trembled as he obeyed the order, sinking into his chair. Was this related to those phone calls he'd been ignoring? If he could convince this hulk of a human that he wasn't afraid, maybe he could get out of this alive. "As I said, I have an appointment with a client on the mainland, but I could pencil you in for sometime this evening. How does six o'clock sound?"

There was no way Braden was going to be back by six. If things went well, he might never come back. He'd use the weekend to disappear while movers boxed up everything for him. And he was more than ready to move on and start his life away from this place. He picked up his pencil and held it over his calendar, waiting for a response.

The man strode over to the desk, his gaze falling on the box of papers. With a wry smile, he flicked the lid off with a meaty paw and started rummaging around.

"Quite the collection you've got here. Where exactly were you planning to go with all this?" The man's mocking tone turned Braden's guts into an acid bath.

Still, he wasn't going to show just how shaken he was. "Those are confidential papers for a client who's waiting, as I've said." Braden leaned forward, ready to snatch the box away from the man. "Please don't touch them."

"That's a pretty little lie. But we both know there's no client waiting for you. In fact, you've been ducking your calls for hours. And our bosses aren't too happy about that."

Our bosses?

Desperation clawed at Braden's insides, his mind racing

with thoughts of self-preservation. This guy could be fishing for information. "I never got an email from them. If you really work for my client," he stressed the word, "and they have a case they want to work on, they should make contact with me in the usual way."

The hulk laughed as he produced a gun from under his jacket, leveling it at Braden's chest. "The Yacht Club has decided that emails aren't personal enough for their current needs. That's why they sent me."

Braden blinked several times, trying to shake himself out of the shock settling into his system. His gaze stayed locked on the gun's silencer, while his brain kept chanting the same thing over and over.

This can't be happening. Not when I'm so close to starting a new life.

He didn't recognize the man, so he was betting he was outside help. Maybe Braden could use that to his advantage.

"Look, let me be frank. I'm sure you've only recently been hired by the Yacht Club. I'm their defense attorney and know every one of their members. So trust me when I say this is not an organization you want to be associated with. They have more enemies than friends now."

The hulk of a man shrugged that off. "I don't need friends. Or even friends of friends. I'm only working for the Yacht Club because they pay me well and I find the work interesting." He flipped through the box of files, acting like he was reading them. But all the while, his focus stayed on Braden, and the gun never wavered.

Braden ignored the growing pressure in his bladder and kept the smile plastered on his face.

"It's only their exterior that's shiny." He tapped the stack of papers that the hulk had been looking through. "Their bank accounts are nearly empty. Members in jail. Members who went to jail but died while waiting for court. These people have no loyalty."

The man didn't even blink. "Why should I believe you?"

Braden frowned, shaking his head. Juries always responded well to this act. "My partner was shot dead in the street while his client hid behind him. If you work for them, you'll end up the same. Like the man before you. Dwight Stokely knew jumping to his death was a kinder way to go than at the hands of the Yacht Club. I'm choosing a smarter way out. One where I'm not looking over my shoulder for the rest of my life. You could too."

"I could?"

Braden grinned, certain he'd won over his would-be killer.

The hulk leaned in, eyes narrowed. "The club's accounts are nearly empty because they sent all their money to me." His lips parted, showing his straight, pearly-white teeth as he drew out that last word. "I'm the person you call when you need a *big* cleanup. And you're the first person on my to-do list."

Ice filled Braden's veins, and his hands started to shake. "Please." His voice was barely above a whisper as he rose from his seat. "I…I have money. I can pay you whatever they paid. And you can tell them I'm dead. Just let me go."

"You'd pay me the same amount of money they're paying me? There's only one problem with that." A thoughtful expression crossed his face. "They won't take me at my word that you're dead. They'll want proof."

Without hesitation, he pulled the trigger. The silenced gunshot sounded like a muffled cough in the small office, but its impact was unmistakable.

Pain seared through Braden's chest as he crumpled to the floor behind his desk. He clutched the wound, desperate to staunch the flow of blood. He looked down. His shirt was red. He had a moment to wonder if he should pretend to be dead. But that plan was foiled as soon as he started gasping for air.

The assassin approached him with an eerie calmness and set a duffel bag on his desk. He tucked the gun away somewhere under his jacket. Donning a pair of gloves, he pulled out a set of tools from the duffel before moving to Braden's computer, which he popped open, removing the hard drive before closing it. Such an easy and neat solution.

Squatting down, the man seemed to be assessing Braden's injuries. "I can be bought. But only by one person at a time. And the deal she gave me is a lot better than what you're offering anyway."

She?

There was only one *she* that could have done this.

Swallowing hard, Braden tried to think of something else to say as the big man pulled a thin knife from behind his back. Braden instinctively tried to move away but failed. It was like his mind and body were no longer connected. Was this shock? His brain trying to distract him from the fatal pain in his chest?

The hulk's meaty fingers wrapped around Braden's jaw and squeezed, prying his mouth open.

In horror, Braden watched the knife enter his mouth. There was a sharp jabbing sensation, minor compared to the agony in his chest, but intensifying in pain as the man began to saw.

"You're not going to need this anymore." Chuckling, the man retrieved Braden's severed tongue from his mouth.

Choking as blood ravaged the hollowed-out space in his mouth, Braden tried to scream. Viscous gurgling sounds were all he could manage.

The man placed the tongue in a clear plastic bag before

wiping his hands with several prepackaged hand wipes and drying them with a towel he'd pulled from his duffel.

After that, the room and the hulking monster before Braden faded to black.

The last sound he heard was the hum of the paper shredder coming to life. A cruel mockery of his failed escape plan.

2

"Rebecca, my parents are the Yacht Club."

Those words echoed in Sheriff Rebecca West's head, as persistent and unsettling as the sterile buzz of the fluorescent lights overhead. The lights cast a harsh glare on the cold metal table separating her and Senior Deputy Hoyt Frost from their prisoner, Ryker Sawyer. As Rebecca locked eyes with Ryker—the man she'd called her boyfriend until last night—her heart ached with a mixture of hurt, sadness, betrayal, and anger.

How could I have been so foolish?

It was one o'clock in the afternoon, but it might as well have been the depths of night in the windowless interrogation room. The only clue that a world existed outside came from the occasional burst of heavy rain pelting the roof.

"Ryker." Her voice was steady despite her roiling emotions. "You know as well as I do that it's time to bring down your parents and the Yacht Club. They tried to get you and Luka Reynold to kill me."

"I wasn't going to kill you. I was told to leave the door

unlocked so Luka could get in, but then I was going to stop him. You heard me tell him to stop." He tried to smile. "That has to count for something, right?"

Her fists clenched under the table. Those damn adorable dimples made him look so sweet. Now she was certain he used them to hide his rotten core. She ignored his comment and his innocent smile. "Count for something? You aided a fugitive murderer to get into my home. You weren't even supposed to be there."

"Rebecca's right." Hoyt leaned forward. "The Aqua Mafia's collapsing anyway. The club's a laughingstock on the island. The boogeyman in the shadows isn't so scary now. Especially since so many of the members have gone to jail or been killed, half of it from simple infighting."

"I always hated it when you called the Yacht Club the Aqua Mafia. It's such a juvenile and demeaning name." Ryker fidgeted in his seat, dropping his focus to his handcuffed wrists.

"It seems fitting for a criminal organization that targets underage girls and whose members act like frat boys on spring break," Rebecca snapped back.

She was hurt, but more than that, she was angry. At him. At his parents. At the fate that had brought her here to this town.

All she'd wanted was a vacation to heal and recover after she'd tracked down her parents' killers and nearly died herself. The space and time to plan her future. Instead, she'd become embroiled in something far more complicated than what she'd left behind.

Hoyt lifted his hand, signaling her to back down. She was only here to get Ryker talking. He was the one who was supposed to be steering the interview. She pulled back, letting him take over.

Lifting his hat from his head, Hoyt ran his hand through

his hair before setting it back down again. "We have Wallace's files, and we're searching several of their yachts as we speak, and it won't take us long to dig through everything on your phone. And we've got Luka Reynold's phone too. But we still need direct evidence that your parents are in charge. Your testimony can change that."

Ryker shook his head, his jaw set stubbornly. "You don't understand. My parents always get what they want. Testifying against them would make me disloyal, and I refuse to be disloyal, no matter what you think of me. You're asking me to crucify myself."

"Disloyal?" Rebecca clenched her jaw tighter. "What about what you did to me? You made me think you cared, tricked me into having feelings for you. I let you and Humphrey move into my house. Your dog is still there because he has nowhere else to go!"

"My dog?" His shrug was so casual, so unnerving. "Humphrey picked sides the day he met you on the beach. And he picked them again during the fight last night. Maybe Humphrey knows me better than anyone. Besides, I already said you can keep him."

He didn't seem to care about the dog any more than he cared about her. Was that what being raised by sociopaths did to a person? As her cheeks heated, Rebecca pushed her chair back to stand. Hoyt shot her a look, forcing her back down into the seat.

She spoke without thinking. "You don't even give a shit about the dog."

Ryker stared at her as if she'd sprouted a new head. "It would've been nice if Humphrey had shown me unconditional love. But he never warmed up to me. And it's not like I tossed him overboard or in the furnace or anything. I'm not as mean as my mom."

Rebecca felt like her eyes would bulge out of her skull.

"Your mom? Tossed him overboard? What are you saying?" She couldn't even force herself to ask about the furnace. Just the idea of Humphrey's sweet face as he was tossed anywhere was enough to make her blood boil. And Ryker spoke like it was the most normal thing in the world.

Ryker's gaze shifted from her to Hoyt as if looking for help.

Hoyt stared at him, his jaw clenched.

"It's not like they treated *me* that bad." Ryker straightened, coming to his family's defense. "When they tossed me overboard, they always made sure there was at least a raft being pulled behind the boat to swim to. And that only happened when they were really pissed off."

So many things were making a lot more sense to Rebecca now, hearing that tiny bit about his childhood. She almost felt sorry for him. In her memories, she could still see the gangly little boy she played seaweed tag with. That same boy would get tossed into the ocean by his parents when he misbehaved.

It was more proof that she never really knew Ryker the way she thought she did.

Something in their faces must've alerted him, because Ryker suddenly shut down. "I need to call my lawyer again. He should've been here by now."

That was true enough. Both Ryker and Luka Reynold had been making calls to their lawyer all morning. None of them had been answered.

"Fine. Deputy Trent Locke will supervise your call." Hoyt stood and looked Ryker up and down with a sneer. "A man like you isn't worthy of a good boy like Humphrey." He motioned for Rebecca to stand.

Those words soothed her enough that she could walk outside without feeling the urge to commit violence.

"You heard him." She spoke as soon as the door was

closed. "He said on the record that I can keep Humphrey." Trent was waiting at the corner by the new metal door to the holding area. Behind that door were the two new cells, one of which was occupied by Luka Reynold. Rebecca waved Trent over.

He held up a landline phone with a lengthy cord. "Does this one want to make a call too? Reynold has been trying all day and says he can't reach his lawyer."

"Yeah, same with Ryker. I can't imagine why their lawyer, or lawyers, would be dodging their calls after they were caught red-handed in the sheriff's house, trying to kill her while she slept." She managed a faint smile, but her mind was elsewhere. "Take that to Ryker. And make sure you stay and supervise him."

"Sure thing, Sheriff." Trent disappeared into the interrogation room.

Hoyt leaned against the wall in the hallway, folding his arms. "Do you think Ryker really believes his parents will protect him after he crossed them?"

"Probably." Rebecca sighed. "The Sawyers don't know their son revealed their involvement. And he seems to be regretting it now. But they have to realize the assassin they sent after me last night failed."

Failed last night. But how many more times will they try to kill me? And how many more people will they hurt in the process? I'm lucky Viviane followed me home and that Humphrey is so fiercely loyal.

"Maybe it's time to show Ryker that devotion works both ways," Hoyt suggested, pulling Rebecca from her thoughts. "Let's see if his parents are willing to protect their son."

"Right." Determination settled into Rebecca's chest. "We need to bring them down once and for all."

As they waited for Ryker's call to end, Rebecca wondered whether the man she had loved could achieve redemption.

She hoped, for his sake, he'd find the courage to defy his parents and help bring justice to the countless victims of their ruthless organization. But one thing was clear in her mind. She would not let the Sawyers slip through her fingers.

Trent emerged, holding the landline. "Ryker wants to talk again."

Rebecca exchanged a knowing glance with Hoyt before they entered the interrogation room once more. The atmosphere was heavy, suffocating, as if the air itself had been stripped of life.

"Lawyer didn't answer." Ryker muttered, his voice hollow and distant. His eyes were downcast, and his hands lay limp on the table. He looked broken, like a puppet whose strings had been cut.

"Want to try someone else?" Rebecca's tone was steady despite the turmoil raging within.

Ryker remained silent, defeated resignation etched across his face.

Of course, Rebecca thought, realization dawning. He'd spent his entire life following his parents' rules, trusting only the people they approved. It made sense that the criminal organization would have a lawyer on retainer. He and Reynold had to be calling the same guy.

Who was their lawyer?

It only took a moment for his name to come to her. Braden Moore.

The tall, well-dressed man who joined Steven Campbell's law firm about a month before Campbell's untimely death back in June. Albert Gilroy's lawyer and obedient guard dog had been killed. With Campbell dead, Moore hadn't missed a beat. He became the sole attorney for the Aqua Mafia. It would make sense he'd be the one they were trying to get ahold of.

"Listen, Ryker." Rebecca forced herself to maintain eye

contact as she took her seat again. "You're in a bad situation no matter what. Cooperation might be your only chance. And it's the least you can do after everything."

Ryker hesitated, biting his lip.

Rebecca found it disturbing to watch him. His every move and mannerism were foreign to her. Was he putting on an act right now? Or was this who Ryker Sawyer had always been?

Hoyt dropped into the seat next to her, leaning back and letting her take the lead for now.

Rebecca leaned forward. "Your parents instilled loyalty into you since birth, but they have no qualms about sacrificing you. Or anyone else. They treat loyalty with contempt. Your only real options with them are choosing between a fast or slow death."

"Actively working against them is a betrayal on another level altogether. They'd make me wish I were dead." Ryker shook his head, his eyes unfocused.

"Unless you provide enough information that they can never find you again."

"Rebecca's right." Hoyt interjected in a firm voice. "If you still don't want to cooperate, maybe a couple of nights in state jail will change your mind. You know what happened to all the other members who went there. They're dead now."

The weight of his words hung in the air like an executioner's axe. Ryker's gaze flickered back and forth between Rebecca and Hoyt, desperation seeping into his eyes. It was clear from his expression that he knew they were right. But could he find the strength to defy his parents?

Considering the way he'd claimed to have been punished as a child, it'd take a miracle for him to be willing. But Rebecca had seen glimpses of a caring person before.

Was that only an illusion?

She had no answer for that question.

"You're not a dog, Ryker." Hoyt clenched a fist. "Why are you protecting people who treat you worse than one?"

Tears glistened at the corners of Ryker's eyes as his head shook.

It was so small a movement, Rebecca wasn't certain if it was him denying Hoyt's words or if he was shaking in fear.

"They made sure there was a boat." His voice was small and strained. "There was always a boat for me to swim to. And I could hide on that until they cooled down. Then, no matter how many days it took, they always pulled me back in. My parents never left me behind. They won't leave me behind now."

Rebecca had no idea what to say in the face of such insanity and pain. *Days?* They'd left him on a small boat being towed behind their yacht for *days*?

What Ryker was describing was torture. Isolation, threat of death, exposure to the elements, possibly sleep deprivation. She'd glimpsed the face of the man she knew so well as he'd spoken those words.

"Ryker. Look around you." Hoyt spread his arms wide. "They did leave you behind. There is no boat. There is no help coming. Your lawyer isn't taking your calls. Why do you think that is? He's their lawyer, too, isn't he?"

He bit his lower lip, keeping his eyes focused on the table in front of him.

Hoyt leaned forward, putting his face close to Ryker's. "And I wouldn't treat my worst enemy the way they treated you when you were only a kid. That's child abuse. Torture. If that happened to an enemy combatant, it would be a war crime. You were just a child. I understand you want to believe your parents are going to pull you back in. But you're not a kid anymore. And your parents are only going to save themselves."

"Fine." The whispered word escaped Ryker's lips on an exhale. "I'll testify."

A bittersweet sense of triumph washed over Rebecca. Maybe there was someone good buried under all the twisted training he'd received. It was a small victory, but one that brought them closer to dismantling the Sawyers' criminal empire. Yet she couldn't shake the sorrow of losing the man she once loved to the monsters they fought against.

"Thank you." Her gratitude was sincere, but her heart felt heavy with the knowledge that no matter the outcome, their lives would never be the same again.

3

Rebecca and Hoyt stepped out of the interrogation room, the fluorescent lights in the hallway casting a pallor over their faces. Trent was waiting, leaning against the wall with his arms crossed. If she'd had more time, Rebecca probably would've taken off to go wash her face until she scrubbed the images of Ryker's torture from her mind.

"How'd it go?" There was genuine concern in Trent's eyes.

"Ryker's agreed to testify." Rebecca's voice was tired and shaky. Fatigue assaulted her like a tidal wave. The events of the past few days, coupled with her lack of sleep and the harrowing fight for her life last night, had left her exhausted.

Her vision blurred, and her knees buckled.

Trent and Hoyt lunged forward to catch her, but Rebecca managed to steady herself just in time. She let out a weak laugh. "I must look pretty bad if you guys think I'm going to keel over. Maybe I should go home." Her joke fell flat as both men still looked concerned. It seemed her sense of humor was as tired as she was.

"Sounds like a good idea." Hoyt glanced at Trent, who nodded in agreement.

"Let me bring the cruiser around." Trent gestured to the door, which led directly to the parking lot. "You get your stuff from your office, and I'll meet you out front."

"Thanks, Trent." She gave him a small, weary smile as he grabbed his raincoat and jogged off to the parking lot.

Hoyt accompanied her to her office, his presence comforting and solid.

"Finish up the paperwork from last night." Rebecca rubbed her temples. "And remind Viviane she needs to do hers too."

Hoyt smirked, raising an eyebrow. "I know how to do my job, Boss. Don't worry about us. Go get some rest."

As they talked, Rebecca retrieved her gun from her desk drawer, slipped on her jacket, and picked up her house keys. The sight of them made her pause, her stomach twisting. Ryker had a copy of her key. What if he'd made more?

Hoyt noticed her fixation and cleared his throat. "Uh, since your old house is a crime scene now, we packed up the rest of your personal things and moved them to your new place. Vi grabbed what was left in the bathroom, and we moved your boxes over. Your truck too. Humphrey too. You don't have to go back there ever again."

Rebecca felt a rush of gratitude at his words, knowing she wouldn't have to revisit the house where Ryker had betrayed her so cruelly.

"You know, Boss, there are less dramatic ways to get people to do all your moving for ya."

Rebecca appreciated his attempt to lighten the mood. "Yeah? Well, I'll remember not to get attacked the next time I want to relocate."

Hoyt escorted her to the front door, where Trent had pulled up in the cruiser. She said goodbye to Elliott before stepping outside. The day was gray, a misty drizzle falling from the sky. Without a word, Rebecca climbed into the vehicle.

The rhythmic thump of the windshield wipers lulled Rebecca to sleep as they drove. She woke with a start when the cruiser pulled in front of her new house. Mumbling her thanks to Trent, she stepped into the damp air and made her way to the front door. Just as Hoyt had stated, her blue truck was parked in the driveway.

The house was identical to the other one, just as Ms. Shuping had promised. As she walked inside, Ryker's chocolate lab bounded up to greet her. Ryker had confessed that he'd only gotten the dog to try to win her over. She was happy to take him. Despite Humphrey's ties to her duplicitous ex, the dog brought her joy and was part of her life now.

His familiar presence brought a small smile to her face. He'd been thoroughly checked out that morning after he'd helped her fight off Reynold. The vet had given him a clean bill of health.

Her joy faded as she glanced around the living room. Boxes were scattered about, a stark reminder of the life she'd left behind.

She couldn't escape the nagging feeling that everything in those boxes was tainted by Ryker's deceit. How could she have been blind enough to let him into her life, to share her home and her bed? Would she ever be able to trust again?

Exhausted, she sank onto the couch and pulled Humphrey close, falling asleep as she had in the cruiser on the way home. But despite the chocolate lab's comforting presence, her dreams were fitful, volleying between flashes of Reynold attacking her and memories of her family vacations.

She awoke with a jolt, her heart racing as she glanced around the room for intruders.

There were none, of course. Only sweet Humphrey, staring at her with his head cocked and that adorable puppy grin.

"Sorry, buddy. Didn't mean to startle you."

Desperate for a distraction, she flicked on the TV. The program choices early on a Friday afternoon weren't great. She chose to ignore the soap operas and courtroom reality programs for a documentary about Bigfoot. Rebecca tried to lose herself in one of her favorite guilty pleasures. But as she stared blankly at the images of shadowy forests and blobby footprints, she couldn't shake the questions that haunted her.

How had she been fooled so easily? And what would happen when the next nice guy came along? She tried to ignore the possibility that she only attracted men who were too weak to deal with her job and her independence.

The shrill ring of her phone pierced through Rebecca's restless thoughts, and she grabbed the device, trying to shake away the fog in her brain. "This is West. Did I oversleep?"

Elliot's apologetic voice greeted her. "I'm sorry to bother you, Boss. There's been a murder. I know you were trying to catch up on sleep, but I thought you'd want to know."

"No. You're right. I want to know." This was what she had been afraid of. The backlash of arresting Luka Reynold and Ryker Sawyer. Jim and Vera were fighting to stay free, and everyone they knew was a potential victim. As soon as she had something she could legally act on, she'd bring them in. Until then, she didn't want them to discover that she knew they controlled the Yacht Club. "Who is it?"

"Braden Moore, the lawyer Reynold and Ryker have been trying to call since being brought in." Elliot spoke with real concern. "He was found dead in his office by the janitorial staff. It's not an old body either. Locke and Hoyt are on their way there now and suggested I call you, considering his affiliation with the Aqua Mafia."

"Thanks, Elliot. And they're right. This is almost certainly because of his ties to the Yacht Club. I'll head over there right away." As Rebecca hung up, an odd sense of relief washed over her. Finally, she had something she could act on instead of waiting on Ryker to deal with his mommy and daddy issues.

She wasted no time in pulling on her shoes and grabbing her jacket. The rain from earlier was still hanging around.

Her mind raced with thoughts of Braden Moore, the tall, pleasant-looking man who'd moved to town in late May. His death could open the door to unraveling the Yacht Club's operations, and she couldn't afford to miss any clues.

Smiling, she ruffled Humphrey's ears and took a moment to let him out to relieve himself. After far too much sniffing, the dog returned at Rebecca's order. He marked some dune grasses before bounding back inside.

As she grabbed her keys to leave her new house, she felt Humphrey's eyes on her, the loyal dog no doubt sensing her unease. She turned at the door. "I'll be back, buddy. And once this weather clears up, I promise we'll go chase the waves on the beach. Okay?"

Humphrey's ears perked up, and his long tail wagged weakly.

She didn't need no stinking man. Not when she had such a loving and adorable dog waiting for her at home.

4

Deputy Trent Locke eyed the janitor, Yolanda Cashion. Standing just inside the open door to one of the only two law firms in town, she was visibly shaken. Her heavyset frame trembled as she recounted her discovery of Braden Moore's lifeless body.

"I...I walked into his office, and there he was, dead on the floor. He was half hidden by his desk, so I made it a couple steps in before..." She stopped, her gaze shifting to Moore's open door. "I called 911 right away, I swear. That poor man."

"Did you know him well?" Trent kept his deep voice steady, attempting to comfort her.

Crouched next to her was Hoyt, taking pictures of Moore's door, lock, and jamb.

"No, not really." Yolanda tried to push back her gray hair, which was stuck to her sweaty forehead. "I barely knew him. He's only been here about six months and kept to himself."

Trent turned to the other witness, Buck Donner, the building's security officer. Tall and thin, he'd been shuffling his feet back and forth continuously since Trent's arrival. "Did either of you hear anything before you found the body?"

Yolanda shook her head. "I come in during Mr. Moore's lunch. So I start on the first floor offices in the morning and then come up here around twelve thirty to clean while he's out." She looked at Donner.

"I didn't hear anything," he mumbled, avoiding eye contact. "I don't know how this happened. I didn't see anyone come in."

"Thanks for your help. We can handle things from here." Trent nodded at them both, tapping the phone numbers he'd taken down on his notepad. "If we have any more questions, we'll come find you."

Cashion scurried off as quickly as she could, but Donner dragged his feet and looked over his shoulder often, guilt sloughing off him in waves. Trent could fully understand that.

He still remembered the day he had to stand over a puking witness after she'd found two decapitated bodies at the old witch's cottage. While he'd done his job the way he was supposed to, he still felt that it was his fault that poor girl had walked into the charnel house.

The what-ifs had played havoc in his mind. That had been the turning point for him, seeing how badly crimes could affect people even if they weren't the intended victims. Somehow, it snapped everything together.

And he'd started taking his job more seriously after that. After all, he'd signed up to deal with things like this. The civilians of the island hadn't. He needed to protect them.

Hoyt had moved on from the doorway and was focusing on the desk. Trent came up beside him. It wasn't pretty, but he'd seen worse since he started acting like a real deputy.

Braden Moore, a once dapper attorney, lay sprawled behind his desk. His hands were limp with death, cupped slightly near his heart, almost hiding the evidence of the fatal shot to his chest. Congealed blood pooled around and inside his mouth.

Hoyt grumbled, rubbing his knees. "Locke, would you squat down and take a closer look at why Braden has so much blood in his mouth?"

Curious at his partner's request but determined to do his duty, Trent pulled on his gloves and knelt beside the body, careful not to touch the blood. As he peered closer at Braden's open mouth, he realized a weird stump was where his tongue should have been.

"His tongue is missing. I've never seen that before. That's gruesome." Trent swallowed hard. Now Hoyt's suddenly "achy" knees made sense. He'd already guessed the senior deputy had faked sore knees to make Trent look at the gore instead.

Hoyt's next words confirmed that. "Dammit. That's what I was afraid of. What kind of sick bastard would do this?"

Trent agreed as he stood, surveying the scene once more. The thought of someone mutilating Moore like that made his stomach clench. He considered the situation, trying to piece together the events leading up to this grisly murder. Cutting out a lawyer's tongue certainly seemed like a message that talking would get you killed. But he didn't think Moore had talked to the sheriff.

There was little doubt about what happened here, even if he didn't know why.

The white shirt the victim was wearing under his tailored suit was marred by dark gunshot residue, indicating that the shooter had been close when they pulled the trigger. The chest-height hole in the wall behind the desk, spattered with blood, showed that Braden had been standing when he was shot. On the clothing and floor, the blood was still red and hadn't had time to fully dry.

Braden had been first shot and then mutilated. He would have fallen after the gunshot, too weak to defend himself from the attacker. It was simply Trent's theory, but he was hopeful forensics would prove him right.

Trent explained his reasoning to Hoyt as he pulled out his camera. He snapped pictures of the victim, focusing on every detail, from the blood-soaked floor to his cupped hands. For his part, the senior deputy snapped pictures of the office's trash cans.

Once Trent was finished, he looked around. Hoyt turned in a slow circle, too, his eyes narrowing as he surveyed the scene.

"Whoever did this knew what they were doing. They took all the trash out with them. There aren't even bags left. It was the same way under the shredder too."

"What do we have here?" Rebecca startled Trent as she stepped into the room.

Rebecca's usually neat ponytail was tangled, and there were strands flying loose around her temples. Dark circles under her eyes and the weary slump of her shoulders signaled how tired she was.

She'd been through hell and back in recent days. Trent glanced at his watch, calculating that only two hours had passed since he'd dropped her off. Life had not been kind to Rebecca since she'd come to their little island. Instead of finding a reprieve, she'd gotten roped into becoming their sheriff instead.

Trent's guilt gnawed at him as he recalled Wallace's death. An event for which he felt partly responsible. His misguided belief that the Aqua Mafia was simply misunderstood had led to sharing with his supposed friends all the "funny work stories" he'd heard on the job.

At the time, it never occurred to him that he was giving

actual criminals firsthand knowledge about active investigations and cases going to trial. In his mind, he'd only been chatting with friends after work. He'd been so screwed up in his way of thinking that he hadn't even known he was screwing up.

Now he knew better and was determined to right his past mistakes. He was driven by a burning desire to prove himself not only to Rebecca, but to the rest of the team. Since he'd started putting in real effort, it felt like they were starting to accept him too. That was something he'd never thought would happen.

"Looks like we found out why Reynold and Ryker's lawyer never answered their calls." Hoyt grunted as he straightened.

Rebecca's gaze finally rested on Braden Moore's lifeless body sprawled on the floor behind his desk. She turned to Trent, her eyes searching his face. "You know anything about Moore's involvement with the Aqua Mafia?"

Trent hesitated, wishing he had more to offer. "Honestly, I'm not sure. I haven't talked to any of them much recently."

Rebecca stared at the corpse. "Do we know why there's bleeding from his mouth?"

"Whoever did this cut out his tongue."

Rebecca didn't even flinch at the idea. She simply gave a tiny nod, as if that made sense. Then she focused on Trent and raised an eyebrow. "What do you make of that?"

"Could be a message." Trent wondered if she was testing him. Greg used to test him all the time, but that happened less often now. Still, he hadn't worked with the sheriff very much until recently. Did she still think he was a total fuckup? The idea of it made his stomach roil.

He'd messed up plenty, and most of the repercussions from that had fallen on Rebecca's shoulders. Other than one brusque dismissal of his complaints, she hadn't really brought it up. That proved she was a much better person than he was. But he was trying.

"If Moore knew too much, maybe someone wanted to make sure he, and anyone else thinking of talking, stayed silent."

"It's also graphic and terrifying. Let's keep this bit of information under our hats. Did the witnesses notice it?" Rebecca looked at both of them in turn, and he and Hoyt shook their heads.

"The security guard never came into the office, according to the janitor who found him. And she didn't come any closer once she saw he was dead."

"Perfect. So if anyone starts talking about a man missing a tongue, we'll know where they heard it from."

Trent gulped but tried to look nonchalant.

"No, I don't mean you or Frost. It'll mean they talked to the killer or someone involved with Moore's death."

He let out a relieved breath. Perhaps she was beginning to trust him. It had been Rebecca who pointed out that none of the guys pumping him for information were ever his friends. And she'd been right.

As soon as he'd stopped talking about work, they'd ganged up on him, jumped him, and shaved his beard off.

He hadn't let any of his facial hair grow out since then. And he hadn't spoken to those guys either. Not that they hadn't reached out—they had, but not to apologize or make things right. Instead, they'd tried giving him orders. Playing along would have meant covering their crimes.

By then, he'd pulled his head out of his ass enough to understand right from wrong, and he'd brought it to Rebecca's attention.

Rather than firing him or filing charges against him, she'd

given him a second chance. Everyone on the force had. Trent woke up every day hoping he'd be able to live up to their faith in him.

"Finish up here and let me know when Bailey shows up." Rebecca waved at Hoyt before turning to Trent, surprising him with an unexpected gesture. "Come with me. We're going to have a chat with the security guard."

Trent shot Hoyt a look, who pointedly nodded at their boss who was walking away. Pocketing the camera, Trent jogged to catch up to her. She didn't look back, which he took as a good sign that she knew he'd follow her instructions. She went downstairs and headed straight to the security office.

Buck Donner looked up as Rebecca walked in after a quick knock, Trent on her heels.

"There you are, ma'am. I've already pulled up the footage you asked for. Got it right here."

Trent glanced at Rebecca, wondering when she'd found the time to do that. And wishing he'd thought of it.

"There are no cameras in Moore's part of the building. I didn't like that, but the original renter, Mr. Campbell, insisted on it for attorney-client privilege." He made a face, and Rebecca snorted.

"That's a fun lie they all like to hide behind. But you found something anyway?"

The security guard straightened, looking far less guilty than he had upstairs. "They couldn't stop us from having cameras outside. So that's what I checked. I knew no one came in the front, so there was only one place to look." He turned his monitor around so they could both see what he'd found. "Watch."

Donner hit play, and they watched a clip showing a muscular, masked man approaching the building with a duffel bag. The view of the camera didn't reach far enough to indicate where he'd come from, since it was pointed down at the door and not angled to view the sidewalk, which was public property.

Trent leaned closer, scrutinizing the figure in the basic black ski mask and gloves, hoping to recognize his build or his gait.

After looking around briefly, the mysterious figure reached up with a pair of wire cutters, plunging the screen into darkness.

"That's the only camera I have for that door, so there's nothing else to go on. But that's got to be your guy. Right?" Donner smiled tentatively.

"Email me that footage." Rebecca handed the man her business card, his smile fading as she turned to Trent. "I'll pull it up back at the station and see if either of our prisoners recognizes our mystery man."

She was halfway through the door when she stopped and shook her head. Turning back around, she addressed Donner. "I'm sorry. That was rude of me. Could you please send that footage to my email? You've been incredibly helpful, Buck."

Donner's sour look faded away, and he smiled. "No problem, Sheriff. You look like you've been through the wringer."

Rebecca laughed, and it sounded brittle.

Trent watched as she tried to smooth her hair. She had a pretty serious case of bedhead and sort of made it worse.

"Yeah, the shit thing is, I feel worse than I look."

"Frost and I'll stay here and process the scene, Boss," Trent offered, eager to prove his worth. "Why don't you go back and take it easy for a bit?"

Rebecca nodded, then turned and left the room, her footsteps echoing down the hallway.

Trent couldn't help but feel empathetic. He knew exactly

what she was going through, having been betrayed by someone she trusted so much. He'd been betrayed by his childhood friends. People he'd trusted enough to let them pick his career for him.

Now he was going to use that career to make sure they couldn't hurt anyone else the way Rebecca had been hurt.

5

As Rebecca pushed open the station door, heavy rain splashed into the lobby. The weather forecast said they were going to be getting several storm cells in the area, but she hadn't expected each one to be so different.

Elliot Ping looked up from his dispatch desk and nodded a greeting. "Afternoon, Sheriff. Think we should commandeer some boats for the rest of the day?"

"I'd rather stay away from boats." Her voice was heavy with fatigue, and she struggled to shake it off. "They never seem to bring me any luck."

She moved farther into the station, spotting Viviane and Jake huddled together near the coffee machine. They turned to greet her as she approached.

"Hey, Vi, how's Meg doing?"

"Still in a coma. But there's a long list of Shadow Island residents taking turns sitting with her. She doesn't need me keeping vigil, and now that Reynold's behind bars, I can focus on work." Worry was etched on her features. "So what's going on with Moore?"

Rebecca hesitated for a moment before divulging all the grim details. Viviane used to be squeamish about such information. Sadly, she'd had plenty of opportunities to get over that since transitioning from dispatcher to deputy. Rebecca poured a cup of coffee, needing to use one of the paper cups since she'd left her travel mug at home, probably deep in one of the boxes.

"Braden Moore was shot dead in his office and had his tongue cut out. We've got footage showing the building was entered by a large, muscular, masked man."

Viviane's eyes widened, and Jake Coffey, the tall ex-Army military policeman who'd transferred to their island from the state police, frowned. "Middle of the day and on camera? Guy's either got buffalo balls or no brains."

Rebecca held up a hand, fending off any questions before they could be asked. "Well, the mask was effective at hiding his features. Talk to Locke and Frost for the rest of the details. I'm going to see if I can get some answers from the Aqua Mafia members we have in lockup."

Grabbing her cup of coffee, Rebecca made her way down the hall, using her phone to retrieve the email with the video footage that was sent to her. She punched in her code to open the door to the holding cells.

The cells were on her right, a narrow walkway in front of them the width of a hallway. Ryker sat on his cot in the cell closest to the door, staring at his hands. For now, she ignored her ex, trying to think of him only as a criminal.

Reynold was in the farthest cell from the door. He was on his cot with his back against the wall, one arm in a sling and the other casted to his elbow. His face showed no emotion, but she sensed the curiosity behind his gaze, which locked onto her immediately.

She turned the phone to Reynold. He stood and moved to the bars so he could see her screen. The clip played on her phone, showing the masked man cutting the camera wire with unsettling ease. Rebecca watched Reynold's expression for any hint of recognition but saw none. "Any idea who this might be?"

He shook his head. "Can't see the guy's face, but he's more muscular than any of the Yacht Club members I know. Looks taller than most too."

Rebecca studied him, gauging his honesty. She had a feeling he was telling the truth, which led her to suspect that the Sawyers might've finally brought in the "outside help" Serenity McCreedy had warned her about. They tried hiring from within and had failed repeatedly, as Reynold had managed to only kill two out of his four targets. Perhaps Jim and Vera Sawyer had brought in an actual professional.

And the man in the video definitely seemed to be a pro. The kill was clean, a bullet to the chest from point-blank range. The casual way the man cut the camera wire suggested it wasn't his first time. Slicing out a tongue seemed like a message. Although Reynold had castrated Vale, he'd admitted to being in a frenzy. This pro appeared unfazed.

She'd underestimated the Yacht Club in the past. She needed to stop letting them surprise her.

Ryker walked over and wrapped his fingers around the bars. "What's going on?"

Though Rebecca didn't want to engage with him, she realized he might be helpful. After all, he'd agreed to testify against his parents and provide information. It was time to put that to the test. She showed him the frame of the video that captured the man moments before he cut the camera wire. "Do you recognize this guy?"

He shook his head. "What did he do? Looks like he broke into an office building."

She ignored his question. "When you were calling your lawyer earlier, was it Braden Moore who you were trying to reach?" She knew who it was, but she wanted to hear confirmation.

His lips tensed before he nodded. It was only a tiny hesitation, but it was enough to let her know he wasn't fully on board with working with the police, despite what he'd said earlier. She wasn't surprised by that. Words were cheap.

Turning away from him, she addressed Reynold. "What about you?"

"Yeah. It was Moore. Why?"

"You've been trying to get ahold of your guy for more than twelve hours. Did you ever get through? Did you get to talk to him? Or anyone?"

"No. No one ever picked up. What's going on?" Reynold was looking anxious, swaying slightly, as if he were about to start pacing.

"Moore didn't answer because he's dead." Rebecca watched as shock registered across the faces of both Ryker and Reynold. She neglected to mention that he'd been alive until a couple hours ago. There was no reason to give them more information than they needed.

"Do you have any idea why your parents might have wanted to kill your lawyer?" Rebecca asked Ryker, her tone firm but not accusatory. "Did he have dirt on them?"

Ryker hesitated before replying. "Yeah, I think so. He came on board shortly before Campbell was gunned down by that psycho. They'd call him when they needed someone to post bail or defend any of our people in court. I think they contacted him through intermediaries, but I don't know specifics about their legal dealings."

"Include that in your testimony." Rebecca wondered if Ryker was being forthcoming. "I'll get you a pen and paper. Write everything you know. This is going to be your last chance." She turned to Reynold. "Unless you know another lawyer, you're probably going to have to settle for a public defender."

Rebecca's shoulders sagged as she stepped back from the holding cells, exhaustion pressing down on her like a lead blanket. The lights in the hallway buzzed overhead, casting a harsh glow that emphasized every ache and pain in her body. She glared from man to man before shutting the door, taking a moment to lean against the wall and catch her breath.

"Hey, Boss." Viviane's voice made Rebecca jolt. The deputy's usual levity was replaced with genuine concern. "You look like hell."

"Thank you. You're not the first person to point that out today. I feel like it too." Rebecca rubbed her neck wearily.

"Why don't you go back home and get some sleep? We can hold down the fort for a few hours. Forensics will have to do their thing first anyway. We can run down the guy in the video."

Clearly, Viviane had gotten updated on the case from either Trent or Hoyt, precisely as Rebecca had urged her to do.

She knew her deputies were right, but the thought of leaving the station when so many pieces remained unsolved gnawed at her. A part of her wanted to keep plowing ahead until everything made sense.

Rebecca shook off the urge. Exhaustion blurred her thoughts, and she wouldn't be any good to the case if she couldn't think straight. She had to trust her team to take care of things while she caught up on much-needed rest. Thanks to countless therapy sessions, she knew what this really was. She was trying to bury herself in work so she could ignore the pain trying to swallow her heart and soul.

But that had never worked. It only made everything worse in the end. After she'd caught her parents' killer, she'd been left a burned-out husk in the hospital needing to heal from a lot more than just a gunshot wound to the shoulder.

"Are you sure?" Rebecca's voice was laced with doubt. "There's a lot going on, between Meg in the hospital and Moore's murder. By the way, we need to give Ryker a pen and notepad so he can write out his testimony."

"Boss, relax." Viviane hooked her arm through Rebecca's and led her toward the bullpen. "We can handle it. You need some rest, or you're going to be useless to us."

Jake must've been listening, because he was watching as they walked in. "We got this, Boss. You can trust us."

Trust. Such a funny and painful little word. Still, she did trust...*them*. Honestly, if she stayed, they'd probably spend more time worrying about her than working on Moore's murder case. And if all hell broke loose, her exhaustion could be a liability and endanger her crew.

"All right." She gently brushed off Viviane's hold on her, giving her arm a slight squeeze before releasing it. "I'll head home for a few hours. But call me if anything comes up, okay?"

"Will do." Viviane crossed her heart, her dark eyes filled with reassurance. "Now get out of here before you fall asleep on your feet."

"Thanks, guys." Rebecca paused at the door, glancing back at them one last time. "And watch each other's backs. Whoever's behind all this is dangerous."

Coffey gave her a firm nod, his pale-blue eyes steady and determined. "Always, ma'am."

With that, Rebecca left the station, stepping out into the cool island air. It felt refreshing against her skin, and she allowed herself a moment to breathe it in deeply, trying to clear the fog from her mind. At least the rain had stopped for now.

Yet as she walked to her vehicle, the bleakness seemed to

press in around her, whispering of secrets yet to be uncovered. And she couldn't shake the nagging feeling that they were missing something crucial, some piece of the puzzle that would bring everything together.

But for now, all she could do was rest, recharge, and prepare herself for the battle ahead. Because no matter how tired she was, Rebecca wouldn't stop until justice was served.

6

Trent sat hunched over his desk, poring through the paperwork spread out before him. The bullpen was quiet, save for the gentle tapping of computer keys and the metronome-like ticking of the clock. It was after one thirty in the morning.

He felt a pang of relief, knowing they were on the verge of finally dismantling the Aqua Mafia and all their twisted operations. If he could help Rebecca navigate the legal processes and successfully bring down this criminal organization, perhaps he could rebuild his reputation as a deputy and wash his hands of them for good.

A tingling sensation made the hairs all over his body stand on end.

What the hell?

He stood up and looked around.

He must've startled their dispatcher, because Melody Jenkins looked up from the book she was reading, concern on her face.

"Did you feel something, Melody?"

"No. Like what?"

He waved at the air and sat back down. "I think my imagination's playing tricks on me. Sorry to bother you."

She didn't look convinced but nodded. "No worries."

"Stay focused, Locke," he muttered, scanning the documents for any potential missteps that might jeopardize their case. *Standard Operating Procedure* was his new bible. He would follow it to a T.

It was vital that nothing he did could be used against them in court, that no evidence would be thrown out. His mind raced with thoughts of failure—improper detainment, fruit from the poisoned tree, incorrect wording on warrants.

He needed to review his study notes at home, to make sure he had every detail locked down. But what if someone saw those notes? Could that be used against him too?

The Aqua Mafia was all too aware of his shortcomings. They'd put him through that subpar training and then praised him when he barely passed. The only reason he'd gotten a job in law enforcement was because they wanted to use him as an easy way to undermine the sheriff's office.

His thoughts drifted to the new memorial plaque in the lobby, the one only recently installed honoring Deputy Darian Hudson and his service to the island…and his country. Lillian hadn't been able to go through photos of her husband to find a suitable one for the plaque. But now a smiling Darian Hudson in full dress uniform from his first day on the job now resided on the wall next to the late Sheriff Alden Wallace's memorial plaque.

His past gnawed at him, but he couldn't let it distract him now. There was work to be done. He still had to finish writing his reports from the crime scene earlier.

Trent filled out exactly two fields on the form before the world exploded.

The sound was deafening. A sharp, high-pitched ring dominated his hearing. Air pressure pushed against his body

like an ocean wave. The sensation disoriented him. He got to
his feet and stared at the floor as if it had betrayed him.

As he struggled to get his bearings, he saw Melody
cowering under the front desk, hands over her head, her
screams barely audible through his diminished hearing.

If she's screaming, she's alive.

The front of the sheriff's office looked strangely normal
except for the strobing alarm lights over the entrance.
Distantly, he heard the accompanying siren, which meant
Melody must've triggered the emergency alert on the
dispatch board. Help would be coming soon.

He mentally counted the number of people in the station.
Him. Melody. Two prisoners.

The ringing in his ears made it difficult to think. He was
okay. Melody was panicking, but she was okay too.

Trent needed to check the prisoners.

His heart raced as he stumbled down the long hallway
toward the jail cells. As long as they were in his custody, it
was his responsibility to keep them safe and secure.

As he passed Rebecca's office, which was kept closed and
locked if she wasn't there, the scent of masonry hit his
nostrils, and he coughed on the dust. His brain tried to piece
the scene together. Masonry dust probably meant a wall had
collapsed. As he made his way to the rear cells, the dust grew
thicker, telling him he was approaching the epicenter.

A bomb? Did someone just blow up the sheriff's office?

He reached the *T* intersection at the back of the station.
To the right was the shorter hallway that led to the back
door. To his left was the tiny stub of a hall passing the
interrogation room and ending at the secure metal door
where the holding cells had been installed.

Trent couldn't see into the holding cells through the tiny
window of reinforced glass that allowed them to monitor
prisoners from the hallway. A cloud of masonry dust hung in

the air, thick as fog. But the particles were falling like snowflakes, and he saw where the wall had fallen.

A breakout attempt. Shit.

It was the only thing that made sense to his stunned brain. A breakout. He had to stop it.

The jail door required both a key card and a code, which he fumbled in his haste.

He pushed the door open and slammed into it shoulder first, but it refused to budge more than a couple inches.

Shoving with his left shoulder, he pulled his gun, ready to defend himself, Melody, and the prisoners.

But the damn door wouldn't move.

"Come on, come on!" Though he shouted, he could barely hear his own voice. The door slid open another inch before catching on something. He looked down.

The explosion had filled the back area with rubble. He'd need both hands to force the door open, so he holstered his gun for the moment.

The door rocked against the full force of his weight, moving a bit. Metal grated against the concrete floor. Trent felt the vibration through his body.

He was in.

Grit burned his nose and throat. He yanked his shirt up over his mouth and nose, trying to filter out the worst of the dust.

Trent scanned the wreckage for any sign of movement. Ryker's cell was the closest. He found the prisoner cowering in his cell, seemingly unharmed but trembling with fear. Ryker's lips were moving, and it took Trent a moment to realize he was mumbling, "I'm sorry, Mother," over and over.

At least he's alive.

The night air was slowly clearing out the dust, and Trent got a good look into both cells.

Alive wasn't a word that could describe the second prisoner.

Reynold, who'd been in the corner cell with two exterior walls, was a flattened heap on his cot, a pile of broken bricks and cinder blocks covering his head and chest. Only his legs and the cast of his right arm stuck out from under the debris, and they weren't moving. Blood trickled out of the cracked bricks in a thin but steady stream to a growing pool on the floor.

Luka Reynold's life was slipping away by the moment—if he was alive at all.

Focus on who you can save.

Hurrying, he reached for his key card to open Ryker's cell door. The interior cell had remained intact, bars still in place. Ryker was still effectively under control, assuming no other walls were on the verge of collapse.

But even though less than two minutes had passed since the explosion, Trent had moved too slowly.

Three men wearing ski masks climbed through the blasted exterior wall at the far end of the holding cell.

Trent pulled his sidearm as they raced toward him over the stony debris.

While the largest of the trio reminded Trent of the man from the law office surveillance footage, the other two behind him were unfamiliar.

The second man held a set of large red bolt cutters.

The third, wearing track pants, carried a black pack that he held away from his body, like it would bite.

More explosives? It has to be.

Trent wasn't about to let them set off another device. He aimed for the leader, lined up his sights, and squeezed the trigger.

"Freeze or I'll shoot." His voice was steady and commanding, yet they continued their advance.

He fired a round. The sound was deafening in the enclosed space.

The man eyed him through the eyeholes of the ski mask and kept coming.

Dammit, he's wearing a vest.

Trent adjusted his aim, going for a head shot, but the man lifted his own weapon—Trent made out the bright yellow of a Taser—and fired.

The prongs hit Trent's upper thigh. Every muscle in his body tightened. He wasn't sure if he got his second shot off.

His body locked up, and he fell onto his back in front of Ryker's cell.

Ryker watched him, and the bastard didn't utter a single word.

Track Pants and Bolt Cutters descended on Trent, pummeling him with fists and boots while his muscles were still rigid. He told himself to take it. In a moment, he'd be able to move, and then he'd have his own go at them.

Before the surging current ended its onslaught, Track Pants kicked his gun from his hand.

The Taser current stopped.

"Get off me!" Trent roared, fighting to break free.

He yanked the prongs from his thigh and managed to kick, roll, and push his way out from under the pummeling fists. But with assailants on either side of him, he couldn't keep an eye on both, so every other blow was a sucker punch he couldn't see coming.

Somehow, he had to get past the flurry of legs and arms swinging and kicking. As Bolt Cutters thrust a foot at him, Trent wrapped both arms around his leg and flipped the man to the ground, briefly exposing a tattoo on his neck. The guy fell with a scream, and Trent managed to clamber onto his knees.

Trent screamed, his voice choked with rage, despair, and

concrete dust. "Back off!" His ears were still ringing from the blows and the explosion.

His screams must've alerted the leader, because he suddenly joined the fray. Moving like a machine, he plowed a fist into Trent's side.

Bolt Cutters took that opportunity to kick him in the back of the leg, and Trent went down once again. It was impossible to fend off all three of them. The best he could manage was to turn his head and body away from each blow to lessen the impact.

Another high-pitched wail mixed in with the sound of the alarms.

Melody was screaming.

"Run, Mel—!"

A boot to the sternum stunned Trent. While his head was still spinning, something wrapped around his wrist—a handcuff—and his arm was jerked over his head.

Trent lashed out with both legs. One of his kicks made contact with Track Pants.

The man swore and stepped back. Then he brought his heel down on Trent's head.

Trent twisted his head down, trying to protect his face against the concrete floor and all the rubble on top of it.

The leader managed to grab Trent's other hand as a bout of coughing consumed him. Collapsing forward, he landed face-first on the floor. Now his tongue was coated with grit.

Both his arms were behind his back and handcuffed together. Kicking his feet, he was able to slither around onto his side, ready to face whatever came next.

"He's down. Leave it. We still need to get the evidence. The chick up front is gone."

Trent's hearing was starting to come back, but everything sounded tinny and weird. He couldn't tell which of the men was talking, but he heard enough to know Melody had gotten out.

The wet night wind still blew in through the hallway from the gaping hole in the wall. No one else was in sight. Another explosion sounded, this time much smaller. He spun his head around in time to see the trio breach the sheriff's blown-open office door. Over the wailing alarm, he thought he heard the sound of metal protesting. *Bolt cutters.* They were in the evidence locker.

Trent spent a minute wiggling around until he was able to sit up by leaning against the wall next to the interrogation room door. But he was choking on all the dust and couldn't catch his breath enough to try to rise.

He turned just as Track Pants came out of Rebecca's office, carrying evidence bags that he promptly stuffed into his duffel.

Scrambling, Trent made an attempt to brace his feet on the slick, dust-covered concrete so he could at least try to slow them down before their escape. Maybe he could drag out his next beating until backup arrived, or he could knock one of the evidence bags away. Anything to screw up their plans.

Yet the muscular leader ignored him as the trio turned away toward the holding cells. "You're lucky you stole the passcodes, pretty boy."

Since their backs were to him, Trent couldn't tell who was talking. Bolt Cutters stood in front of Ryker's cell, fiddling with something. There came the distinctive beep indicating he'd unlocked the door.

Bolt Cutters and Track Pants seized Ryker, pulling him from his cell.

The leader picked up a yellow pad from the cell floor. He swiped the masonry dust off and scanned it for several long moments, his fist tightening by his side. "What the hell's this?"

To give him a tiny bit of credit, Ryker didn't flinch as the bigger man grabbed his shirt and shook him.

Trent cursed himself for not taking Ryker's written statement from him earlier. He struggled against the dusty concrete, trying to push himself to a standing position without drawing any attention.

"Barely twenty-four hours, and you're already singing like a canary! This had better be all there is to it, or we're going to have to teach you a lesson too."

Track Pants and Bolt Cutters hauled Ryker and the duffel out of the cell, back over the rubble, and out the blown-out wall.

But the largest one, the leader, stopped at Reynold's cell. He now had the red bolt cutters in his possession.

With the outside wall blown out, the muscular man climbed over the mess into Reynold's cell and approached his lifeless body.

"Leave him alone." Trent's voice sounded like an echo in his head. He still couldn't get purchase against the floor. Still couldn't fully catch his breath.

"Mind your business." The leader bent over Reynold and took several violent snips, each jerk of the cutters eliciting a muffled cry of anguish from under the rubble.

He's alive.

Trent's stomach turned, but he pushed harder, sliding his back up the interrogation door.

The leader had managed to cut through Reynold's cast. He threw the bolt cutters through the massive hole in the wall and withdrew a shiny cleaver from inside his coveralls.

"Stop!" Trent brought all the authority he could muster to that one word as he failed to get his feet solidly underneath him.

Raising the cleaver high over his head, the man brought the blade down against Reynold's exposed wrist. The sickening crunch of bone combined with Reynold's muted scream echoed through the cell.

A second blow from the cleaver freed the hand from his body completely. Blood gushed from the wound.

Moments later, as quickly as he'd arrived, the man vanished into the night. They'd taken their evidence, Ryker, and Luka Reynold's hand with them.

7

Rebecca's sleep was shattered by a shrill alarm from her phone. She fumbled for the device on her nightstand, her mind foggy and disoriented. The harsh light of the screen drew her attention to the words *EMERGENCY AT STATION* followed by a series of numbers and letters.

It took her a moment to understand what she was reading. The code was for her station and was the emergency distress signal from the dispatch board that went to all connected law enforcement units.

Rebecca bolted out of bed, pulling on her uniform as her heart pounded in her chest. The whole time, she chastised herself for thinking she could keep a high-value prisoner like Ryker in her tiny little station. She didn't need to know the specifics of the situation to know it was bad. No one at the station would've triggered that alarm for anything but the direst of reasons.

Grabbing her keys and work belt, she raced to her truck. Driving forward, she pulled through her yard and sped toward the police station, maneuvering the vehicle like it was government owned. She didn't see any flames licking up into the rain. That was one good thing.

As Rebecca pulled up to the station, the scene that greeted her was confusing.

A gray haze hung in the air, mixing with the light rain that had been falling since yesterday. As she parked in front near the downspout, she got a good look down the side of the building, where a strange light filled the alley. It took her a moment to figure out where it was coming from.

There was a massive hole in the side of the building. Rebecca climbed out of her truck and pulled on her utility belt with practiced ease. The air reeked of gunpowder.

Her hackles immediately went up. She scanned up and down the road. She was the first responder there, and there was no movement except for the falling rain and swirling lights approaching from the distance.

"Rebecca," a weak voice croaked from behind her.

She turned and found Melody coated in gray dust and coughing, crawling out from behind her car. The experienced evening dispatcher appeared wide-eyed and pale. Or that could've been from the gray dust coating her skin.

"What happened?" She rushed to the woman and held her elbow, supporting her as she rose.

"N-not sure. Need to sit." Melody's legs gave out before she'd gotten fully upright. Rebecca helped her back down to the ground and crouched beside her.

A fire truck screeched to a halt, its lights casting an eerie glow over the wreckage.

Rebecca waved the responders over, pulling her keys from her pocket. A firefighter knelt beside Melody, and Rebecca asked him to monitor her just as a cry for help came from inside the station.

Scrambling to her feet, she rushed to unlock the front

door. This wasn't an accident. There could still be attackers inside. She didn't want any of the fire crew to get hurt.

Pulling open the front door to the station, she glanced back. One firefighter held his arms out wide, holding back three more in turnout gear. The one attending Melody had her on her feet now, and he was escorting her away from the station. Rebecca held her hand up, telling the others to wait for her to clear the building. With her gun drawn, she stepped inside.

"Help!" Trent's voice reached her ears over the wail of the alarm.

Rebecca's heart pounded as she approached the half door separating the lobby from the back of the station. She squinted, trying to see through the haze, which she now realized was dust, not smoke or gunpowder. The front door swung open behind her. She turned to find Viviane, her own gun drawn.

"Darby, on me," Rebecca ordered, her tone urgent.

Crouching low, she moved cautiously through the station, Viviane a pace behind and off to one side. Together, they cleared the bullpen and locker room. She approached her office door. It stood open, and she and Viviane cleared her office before continuing down the hall.

At the *T* intersection at the end of the hall, she saw a pair of legs to the right, splayed on the floor. Slowing, she stepped left to get a better view. Her heart raced as she crept closer, recognizing Trent's familiar form. He was leaning against the wall, his hands behind his back, softly moaning.

Before she could move to help him, she looked to the left, verifying the holding cells were empty.

Why the hell did they blow down a wall instead of breaking down the back door or even just picking the lock? Who the hell are these people?

Squatting, she tapped Trent's leg and he jerked away.

"Trent, it's West. Are you okay?"

"Boss." Trent's voice was gravelly, and each breath was accompanied by a wheeze. "Area's clear. They're gone."

She refused to put her gun away and nodded for Viviane to uncuff him.

As she did, his wheezing eased. With Viviane's help, he managed to get to his feet. He swayed for a moment but caught himself with a hand on the wall. Blood streaked down his face, and he coughed violently.

"I need to check the jail cells. Wait here." Rebecca tried to step around him.

"Stop." Trent croaked, grabbing her arm. "The wall's unstable. There's no one alive in there anyway."

Rebecca's blood ran cold, her mind refusing to process what that meant. Trent's coughing worsened, and he nearly collapsed. Viviane supported him, guiding him toward the front of the station while Rebecca watched their backs.

As they neared the lobby, Hoyt entered in his hastily donned uniform.

"Take Locke. He needs medical." Rebecca motioned for Viviane to pass Trent to Hoyt. "Darby, you're with me."

Viviane nodded and moved up beside her. Even if there was a gaping hole in the wall, she still needed to secure the station as best as possible. Taking Trent's warning to heart, Rebecca approached the jail area again but didn't enter. Instead, she pulled the door closed and made sure it locked.

After that, she and Viviane cleared the rest of the station to make sure no one was hiding inside. The last room was the new unofficial lounge where the old table and couch were stored. This space was barely big enough to hold the furniture and was on the opposite end of the hall from the new holding cells. As they finished checking that room, her anxiety finally dropped down to a ten from the eleven it had been.

"I need to check on Locke and Melody." Rebecca turned and jogged out of the building, trying not to trip or kick up too much dust. On the off chance the forensic techs could salvage a shoe print, or even a partial, she did her best to watch where she stepped.

As she pushed out the front door, the first person she saw was the fire marshal, Gil Bentley. They'd worked together when three boats had gone up in flames a couple months earlier. "The building is clear, but the back eastern wall has a giant hole in it. I didn't see any smoke or fire."

"We've given your people oxygen to help with their breathing. As for the building, we still need to check to make sure nothing catches on fire. The gas company's been notified, and they shut off the main near here."

Rebecca waved them inside. They were the experts, and she wasn't going to get in their way as they performed their safety assessment.

Hoyt was standing next to his truck as a light drizzle trickled off his hat. Melody, wrapped in a blanket, seemed otherwise unharmed as she huddled in the passenger seat to stay dry. Trent was sitting behind the steering wheel, holding an oxygen mask to his face. His eyes, fixed on Rebecca, were filled with defeat.

She walked over.

"Check the wall on the side of the building." His voice was a raspy whisper through the plastic mask. "They blew a hole in the wall. I tried to get to the prisoners, but they came in and stopped me. Reynold was near dead from the explosion. Ryker was alive."

Rebecca waited while another coughing fit racked him. "Where's Ryker now?"

"They took him," Trent continued. "And Reynold's hand. He's gotta be dead now."

"Are you certain he's dead?" Rebecca needed to know if this was a rescue mission or not.

"He was already dying from the explosion and the weight of the debris on him. The blood loss from his hand…" Another coughing fit overtook him.

"Frost, check the alley and keep watch down there. Coffey's pulling up now. Darby, have him set up a perimeter the firefighters think is reasonable and keep an eye out for anyone suspicious."

Rebecca brushed her hair back and realized Trent and Melody weren't the only ones covered in grit. Thankfully, the rain was already washing her clean.

"Big guy from Moore's office," Trent choked out, holding up fingers as he counted three of them. "There was also a dude wearing track pants who looked like a football player past his prime and a scrawny guy about my height carrying bolt cutters." That was all he managed to say before dissolving into another coughing fit.

As Rebecca waited for Trent to compose himself, Greg Abner pulled up in front of the building. He rushed over to where his colleagues huddled inside Hoyt's truck. Firefighters were now streaming in and out of the building, shouting updates to each other, but Rebecca tuned them out, focusing instead on getting as much information as she could.

Greg got on one knee to examine Melody, but the night shift dispatcher waved him off and pointed to Trent. Melody looked up at Rebecca, her eyes wide with shock.

"What happened?" Rebecca asked, her voice steady despite the turmoil swirling within.

Melody's voice trembled as she recounted her experience. "There was an explosion. It shook the floor, and the lights briefly flickered. It was so loud. I hid under my desk. I don't know how long it took me to get up and hit the emergency button on the switchboard. Then I stayed under my desk until I heard Trent tell me to run. So I took off. I felt like a coward leaving him behind, so I didn't make it very far."

"You shouldn't. Trent is a trained deputy. It's his job to get you to safety. I'm glad you listened to him, or this could've been much worse."

While Rebecca took Melody's statement, Greg moved on to Trent, wiping the dust from his face and assessing the damage. Swollen spots that would surely become bruises marred his skin, along with several small cuts.

With a dirt-streaked face, Trent actually looked his real age of early forties. In one hand, he held a cup of water. The oxygen mask was in his other. Trent leaned out of the truck to spit in an attempt to clear his airway.

He took a deep breath. "I checked on Melody first. I heard the alarms and tried to help her."

Rebecca nodded, understanding the significance of his actions. When Trent had been the old sheriff's backup, he'd failed to check on his fallen partner, leading to Wallace's death. That wasn't a mistake he'd made this time.

"Then what happened?" Rebecca rubbed her throbbing temple.

Trent's voice grew even more strained. "I ran to the back, unlocked the holding cell door, and was attacked by three men wearing masks."

An ambulance pulled up near them, and Greg waved to get the attention of the EMTs.

Trent coughed again, wincing in pain. Rebecca's face softened with sympathy.

"Get checked out," she told him gently. "We'll get your full statement later." She turned to Greg. "Frost's down the alley, keeping watch. Can you step over there and help him until more backup arrives from the state police? Just be careful of the wall. It's unstable."

Greg nodded. As he moved away, Rebecca made a quick detour to her cruiser. She grabbed her camera and went back into the building.

Switching the camera to video mode, she did a slow walk through the chaos that had once been a pristine, renovated police station. By now, the gray dust from the explosion had mixed with rainwater tracked in on boots, creating streaks of cement-like sludge that caked her boots as she filmed. The air was already improving as the humidity from outside seeped in.

"Bentley, we believe we have a body in there, Luka Reynold, and he's under a pile of debris."

"Good to know. I'll pass the word to my team."

"So what's the damage?" She stepped up next to the fire marshal, who was surveying the scene with a practiced eye.

"Thankfully, there's no fire and no gas leaks." He looked over at her, his face still mostly hidden by the respirator he wore. "You really shouldn't be in here for long. The air quality's crap. And at this point, we can't say for sure whether the wall is stable or if any of the roof will cave in. That will be the county engineer's call."

"I'll be quick." Rebecca nodded, understanding the precarious situation. "I'm not going to play Rambo here. I just need to do my job."

He grunted but didn't protest as she walked down the hall.

She saw why her locked office door was open. The door was hanging crazily, a fist-sized hole showing where the doorknob with its new locking mechanism should've been. When she'd cleared the space earlier, she hadn't taken the time to assess the destruction.

The evidence locker stood open. The bags of evidence and Reynold's and Ryker's personal belongings were gone.

The corner of the wall behind her desk leaned in more than it should, but still looked fairly stable.

Her jaw clenched with frustration, but she pushed that aside for now, knowing she needed to focus on the task at hand. After double-checking to make sure the back wall was intact, she sat at her computer and retrieved the surveillance footage from that night.

As she viewed footage from the cameras in her office and the jail cell, the attack unfolded on-screen. Three men entered the station from the alley after Trent had walked into the holding area. One man, slightly smaller than the others, cautiously carried a black bag.

It probably held the bombs they used on my door and the evidence locker.

Rebecca paused the video, studying their physiques. One intruder was the same man who had killed Moore. He appeared professional and calm throughout the process, while his two accomplices seemed nervous.

Even when Trent shot him in the chest—and he had to be wearing a vest, gauging by the outline under his shirt—he didn't flinch. He also had a Taser, which he pulled out smoothly and used on her deputy.

She watched as they knocked down Trent and kicked him repeatedly while he tried to fight back. But he was outnumbered and outmatched. He managed to get to his feet at one point, but then they all ganged up on him again before knocking him down and handcuffing him. She sped up the footage until they came back into view, and her stomach twisted as she saw them take away Ryker and his statement.

Lastly, she watched the muscular man hack off Reynold's hand, bile rising in her throat at the gruesome act.

Switching to the camera in her office, she watched as the door rocked and the handle was blown onto the floor. The burly looking guy they'd seen at Braden Moore's office stepped in. He took the bolt cutters from the scrawny guy and made short work of the hinges on the evidence locker. The contents of the evidence locker quickly made its way into his bag, which he then slung over his shoulder.

From there, she knew by the time stamp, they left.

None of this was good, but she took solace that they hadn't taken the recordings of Luka's and Ryker's confessions. Now she just had to get them to the Commonwealth's Attorney before the thieves realized they'd missed something.

Rebecca backed up all the information, including the surveillance footage, and went outside. The state police and the bomb squad had arrived, and Melody and Trent were both being looked over by EMTs in the back of the ambulance.

Trent's face was a mix of pain and determination, clearly eager to begin the investigation.

She held up her hand before he could say anything. "Locke, I'm not playing. I don't care if you think you feel up to staying. You and Melody both need to get your asses to the hospital and get checked out. Explosions can mess up your innards, dust can damage lungs, and your ears might be affected too. I want you both thoroughly examined."

Trent choked back whatever words he'd been about to say and glanced over at Melody, who was wide-eyed with fear.

Rebecca kept her voice firm. "There's nothing for you to do here. We've got this. Get out of here and don't make me say it again."

She turned to address everyone else on the scene. "Abner, Frost, can you help get the staties set up? The rest of you, go home. Let the firefighters deal with the aftermath. Get some rest. Tomorrow's going to be one hell of a long day." Pulling her fingers through her limp and crusty ponytail, she sighed.

"I'm going to get cleared by the EMTs, then I'm going home to take a long, hot shower."

Everyone agreed with their marching orders, except Trent, who tried to argue before he started coughing again and had to relent to his body's demands.

Rebecca was happy she didn't have to debate her directive, because she was in no mood to deal with anything else tonight.

Her key witnesses and evidence were gone, her plans upended, and an annoying worry for Ryker gnawed at her. Had he planned this? Was he only playing her, biding his time?

It seemed like something he would do, now that she was seeing him for who he was.

8

I sat in the darkness of the boat cabin, my fingers tapping rhythmically on the table as I listened to the soft lapping of water against the hull. The darkness didn't bother me. I was used to hiding and knew every inch of my boat intimately. Anchored a safe distance from the island's southern tip, I felt secure in the temporary haven.

"Are you sure Archer can pull this off?" Jim, my husband and faithful lap dog, whispered into the gloom. He wasn't as comfortable with the darkness, and his voice betrayed the unease that crept into his soul when the lights went out.

"Moore's death was smooth and professional. Not only is the canary unable to sing, Archer shredded everything in the office and took the idiot's hard drive. He seems eager to please me." I envisioned the man blowing up the sheriff's station and cutting off Luka Reynold's hand as I'd directed. Moore's tongue had been an excellent addition to my collection. I savored the thought of how willing the hired gun was to please me. "He's an excellent plaything."

"That's all you're thinking about?" Jim laughed. Whatever

else he was about to say was drowned out by the approaching hum of a speedboat.

My blood pressure spiked at the sound. I slid my hand under the cabinet with practiced ease, my fingers brushing against the cold metal of the gun I kept hidden there. Yet as the boat drew nearer, I recognized the sound of one of my own seacraft and knew Archer was returning.

"Stay put. I'll handle him." After running my hands through my hair, I was satisfied with my appearance. Archer was the hottest new blood I'd seen in a while. Jim dutifully opened the door and waved me through. My heart quickened as I moved onto the deck to greet my visitor.

The motorboat rocked the ship as it docked.

I waited for Archer and Ryker to climb aboard.

A few minutes later, Archer's broad shoulders nearly blocked out the sight of my pathetic son, who was slumped behind him. Both of Ryker's cheeks were swollen, and one eye was nearly shut.

Were the injuries from a beating or from the explosion? I couldn't tell. Either way, a perverse thrill ran up my spine. It was a fitting punishment for failing to obey me.

"Luka's dead. I got these for you." Archer held up two bags in his right hand. One was an evidence bag, while the other was nylon. Blood pooled along one corner of the second bag and dripped onto the deck.

"I also found this and decided to bring it with me." Archer smirked at Ryker, who kept his head respectfully bowed. I took in the legal pad Archer was holding, and my anger tamped down my arousal. Of course I recognized my son's handwriting, even in the dark. "I'll deal with that later."

Ryker flinched, trying to cower behind Archer, but he stepped aside, pushing Ryker forward to stand on his own.

"Where are Griles and Coach?" I snatched the nylon bag, opening it and reaching inside. My fingers intertwined with the lifeless, limp digits of the dismembered appendage. It was cold, which made me hot.

"Did their part and went home." Archer watched me, his breath quickening. I cared little if it was from disgust or arousal. I could work with either one and had done so often. "Griles wasn't too eager to meet you two. He was nervous the whole time. Even said we might be going too far with attacking a government building like that."

"Interesting." My grip was an unforgiving vice on Luka's hand, the flesh and bones squishing under my might. "Thank you for the intel. We'll keep an eye on Jay Griles and Coach John Brighton. But first, what am I to do with the one you brought back to me?" I nodded toward Ryker.

Archer shoved him onto the cabin floor.

He moaned in pain.

I glared down at my disappointing offspring, wondering where my training had gone awry. "You're a failure, Ryker. The one thing we asked of you, and you couldn't even manage that. Were you about to sell us out?"

Guilt shadowed his battered face as he peered up at me, daring to make eye contact. The truth was in his eyes, but I needed to hear it.

"Did you already tell your whore about us?"

His silence spoke volumes.

Anger overcame me, and I kicked him. "I knew you were a failure as a son, but selling us out? They'll be coming for us directly now."

I needed to account for his betrayal and calculate our next moves. It would take a few days to tie up loose ends before we'd be able to vanish. At least our boat was well hidden for the time being.

"Get up," I spat in Ryker's swollen face, "and pray that your duplicity hasn't cost us everything."

Silence hung thick in the air, punctuated by the gentle

lapping of water against the boat and Ryker's shallow, pained breaths.

Archer's gaze shifted between Ryker and me before he finally broke the tension. "Do you want me to kill him?" His voice was steady and almost indifferent. I found it mesmerizing. He was so matter-of-factly willing to do whatever I commanded.

Pushing aside my carnal thoughts, I glared at Ryker. He both angered and saddened me. As much as his betrayal was despicable, he was still my creation. I couldn't order his death. Not yet, at least. "No." I hated the slight waver in my voice. "No matter what he's done, he's still my son. A mother's burden is eternal."

"You're ungrateful. Do you see how much she puts up with? And you were so ready to turn your back on her." Archer's voice dripped with contempt. "You don't deserve the family name. Most people would kill for a mother as understanding and forgiving as yours."

Archer's words soothed my anger. Clearly, his own upbringing had been far from idyllic, which only made his loyalty more precious. This kind of devotion couldn't be bought—it had to be earned...taught.

"All right." My words silenced Archer's tirade. "Ryker, go speak with your father. He's been planning a punishment suitable for your latest failure. And I have things I wish to discuss with our new man here."

As Ryker scampered away, a strange sense of pride shot through me. We might be a fractured family, bound by blood and secrets, but we would survive this together. Or I'd make everyone regret attacking us.

9

Morning sunlight glinted off wet grass as Rebecca pulled her SUV up in front of the home Trent Locke had inherited from his mother. Greg parked his car just ahead of hers, rubbing his tired eyes as he stepped out to greet her. Six hours in a row of sleep combined with the fresh morning air had done wonders for Rebecca. She was no longer weighed down by sleep deprivation.

Greg didn't look like he'd gotten the same rejuvenating treatment.

"Morning, Abner." She tried to hide a smile as the breeze turned his tousled gray hair into a bird's nest. "I have to admit, I'm surprised you suggested Locke's place as our temporary HQ."

Greg returned her smile with a grunt, attempting to pat his hair down. "Just wait until you see what's inside."

That was certainly cryptic. Together, they walked up the front path, past Viviane's and Hoyt's cruisers. Everyone had moved their personal vehicles down the road and then taken a cruiser home last night to clear the parking lot.

Before they had the chance to knock, Trent swung open

the door, a cautious look in his dark eyes. Rebecca noticed
the doorbell camera mounted on the trim of the door. That
was an extra layer of security she hadn't anticipated.

"Come on in." Trent beckoned them inside.

Greg stepped over the threshold without further
prompting.

Curiosity got the best of Rebecca, and she turned her
head. There was another security camera right under the
eaves at the corner of the house, pointing at his driveway.
She looked the other way and spotted a third camera, this
one pointed along the side of the house.

As she stepped into the foyer, her gaze fell on an arsenal
of weapons lining the walls behind safety locks. There were
rifles, shotguns, pistols, and even a few antique firearms.

Unease crept down her spine. Being surrounded by such
an open display of guns didn't make her feel more secure. If
anything, it made her wonder if Trent had overcompensated
for his previous inadequacies as a deputy.

"Are you okay, Locke?" Rebecca didn't bother hiding her
concern as she took in his bruised and battered face.

He nodded, managing a weak smile as he turned away
from her. Leading the way into the house, he gestured for
her to have a seat. There was a couch along one wall where
Viviane and Greg were seated, two armchairs that were
empty, and a loveseat forming a haphazard and broken circle
around a coffee table. A pot of coffee had been set up on a
tray with coffee mugs and a bowl of sugar.

Trent was doing his best to be welcoming, and it wasn't
half bad.

"Yeah, Melody and I went to the hospital to get checked
out. Like you said. They gave us breathing treatments and
cleared us to go back to work. This is all just superficial,
nothing that would stop me from doing my job." He paused
before adding, "Melody's fine, too, only shaken up."

Rebecca tried to focus on the task at hand, but her mind kept drifting back to the wall of weapons. It didn't take long, though, before her thoughts turned to Luka Reynold. "The fire marshal told me they got Reynold's body out from under the rubble. His body was shipped off to Bailey for the once-over. And I had Abner personally deliver the recorded confessions from Luka and Ryker to the Commonwealth's Attorney."

Hoyt ignored her update, clearly agitated as he focused on Trent. "Is there anything else you want to tell us about what happened last night? Seems kind of convenient they left you alive."

Trent looked taken aback, clearly embarrassed. "What do you mean?"

Hoyt didn't mince words. "The Aqua Mafia's the whole reason you have this job in the first place. They pressed Wallace to hire you after getting you all the certs you needed. Any chance you recognized those guys? Knew anything about what was going to happen? Gave them some intel about the setup of the station?"

Rebecca watched as Trent's face flushed an even deeper shade of red. She wasn't convinced he was involved in any way, but she was curious to see how he would respond.

"The setup of the station? Man, everyone on the island knows the basic layout. It's a sheriff's station. I think they could figure out that the jail cells would be in back without even needing to be inside." Trent's insistence wavered with emotion. "But I swear, I have no idea who those guys were."

Rebecca couldn't tell if he was nervous at getting called out or simply embarrassed about his former affiliation with the Aqua Mafia. She leaned toward the latter.

"Not to mention," Greg waved his hand as if shooing away the thought, "the renovation was the talk of town during the campaign and after. Just like Hugh's place was after he painted the walls. People like to talk about new things. I've had a guy who asked about the two cells in back and how many it could hold because he was razzing his drunk friends at the bar."

Rebecca knew that bit was true, as she'd heard people talking about the additions to the station at the grocery store as well. "Can you give us any details about the men? Have you remembered anything else since last night?"

"Through all the dust, it was hard to see anything at all." Trent's voice grew steadier the more he talked. "The first time I got a good look at one of them was after the Taser stopped, and it was a close-up of a gloved fist." He tapped the lump on the side of his face. "I'd be guessing if I attempted to describe its appearance, though. It was too close to see, the air was hazy from the bomb, and I couldn't hear. But that's what I imagine ogre fists feel like."

Hoyt started looking uncomfortable.

"The second view was pretty much the same as the first. Four gloved knuckles. I know there was a thumb in there somewhere. They were black gloves, if that helps. I could probably draw out the pattern of his shoes, though. After that, I got my first look at their faces. They had ski masks on, the basic black kind. I think. They were covered in dust by then. I wasn't able to catch their eye color."

"What else?" Viviane leaned forward in her chair.

Trent jerked around to look at her but didn't say anything.

"Trent, we don't have an after-action report." Viviane waved her hands around the cozy front room, gesturing toward the handful of people in it. "This is all we have. Only us and what you remember. So give us everything you have, the same way you would for the report if we had access to the forms."

His desperation to help was palpable, and Rebecca found herself feeling a pang of sympathy for him.

"Give him a minute. He's had a rough night and probably only got home a bit ago." Rebecca turned so she was directly facing the deputy. "Close your eyes. Go back to the minutes before the bomb went off. If you can't remember something, that's fine. I was in there after things started settling down, and it was pretty hard to see. It had to be a lot worse right after the explosion."

Viviane nodded in agreement.

When Trent did as she asked, she was able to get the entire sequence of events out of him.

"All of them had black ski masks and black fabric gloves. When I knocked the smallest one down, he had what looked like a tattoo on his neck."

"Okay, good. We're getting somewhere. Anything else?" Rebecca wanted to keep him calm to help him recall the details.

Trent dropped his head in his hands, then jerked as if he'd touched a live wire. "You're lucky you stole the passcodes, pretty boy."

"What?" Hoyt bolted upright.

"That's what the big guy said. When he was unlocking Ryker's cell. 'You're lucky you stole the passcodes, pretty boy.'"

Rebecca shuddered. "Ryker's pal Larry was the one who set up the passcodes and the card readers for the 'employees only' areas, such as my office, the holding cells, and interrogation. Since they blew open my office door, I guess Ryker didn't get all the passcodes. Still…" She was horrified at the thought.

Hoyt was the only one who managed to make a sound. The others sat there staring. "Larry and Ryker share a workshop. Ryker had access to the locks before they were even installed."

"We need to change all of them. We'll hire someone from the mainland this time." The feeling of betrayal settled heavily over Rebecca's shoulders. How many more things would she later learn were compromised by her relationship with Ryker? He'd been allowed nearly unfettered access to the station while they were dating. "That explains how they were able to get him out. I couldn't tell from the surveillance footage."

"You already checked the cameras?" Trent perked up.

"Yeah, but as you'd expect, they didn't catch much. Which was why I was hoping you'd seen more." She pulled out her phone and handed it to him. The surveillance footage from the station was already queued up. "Maybe you can take a look at this and see if you can figure anything out."

She watched as Trent's eyes narrowed in concentration while he played the videos and studied the screen. The others huddled around him as they, too, searched for any detail that could help their case.

As the video played, Trent spoke up. "Wait, pause it there." He tapped the screen to freeze the frame and pointed at the dark lines poking up from the man's collar. "That's the tattoo I saw."

"Sure looks like one." Hoyt leaned over, and Trent zoomed in.

"Does anyone recognize this?" Trent shifted the phone to allow everyone a better look.

The group exchanged uncertain glances, each shaking their head in turn.

Trent peered at the screen again. "I don't recognize that specific tattoo. There's not a lot to see. But I do know someone in the Aqua Mafia with a lot of ink. His name is Jay

Griles. He's covered in tattoos. Also, the body type matches him."

"Could be worth checking out." Rebecca weighed her options, then looked at Hoyt.

"Actually, Boss, I'd like to come with you." Trent jumped in before she could start handing out assignments.

Hoyt's brow furrowed, and he shot Trent a hard glance. "Jay's a former friend of yours, isn't he? It wouldn't be right having you there when we question him."

"We were never friends. I know you don't trust me, but if the boss can interview her ex-boyfriend, I think I can be trusted to sit in on an interview with Griles." Trent shook his head, his voice firm. "I barely knew the guy, and hell, I'm practically old enough to be his dad."

Rebecca studied the two men, pondering their lingering discord. After a moment, she made her decision. "All right, Locke. You make a good point and can come with me. Frost, you go with Darby. I want you to head to the station and check in with the staties down there. Make sure everything is secure."

Standing, Rebecca motioned for Trent to accompany her. He jumped up, and they were out the door and climbing into her SUV.

"Let's get one thing straight," Rebecca said, her eyes locked on the road ahead as she maneuvered the cruiser onto the asphalt. "If you're coming along, we need to follow SOP to the letter. I'm not going to let these assholes slide on a technicality."

Trent nodded, his jaw set in determination. "I won't let you down, Sheriff."

10

Rebecca rolled to a stop in front of Jay Griles's stately house. Though Trent hadn't known the address, it had been easy enough to look up. The pristine white walls of the mini-mansion acted like a beacon, shining through the morning fog as a light rain started again. It sat at the edge of Oyster Bay with a private dock and boat bobbing gently in the water.

She turned to Trent, who was staring at the property with a mixture of awe and distaste. "All right, what do you know about Griles?"

Trent shook his head. "Not a ton. We didn't interact much. But from what I know of him, he's an asshole. Full of himself. Loves bragging about his sexual exploits, like he never outgrew his teenage years."

"What else?"

He frowned. "I saw him on the beach a few times, which is why I noticed the tats. Honestly, I always just saw him as someone's kid cousin that hung out with the older generation to try to look cool."

Rebecca nodded. That was how all these younger Aqua

Mafia members seemed to her. Like kids desperately trying to stand out and get some kind of attention. Which was yet another reason why she'd never suspected Ryker of being one of them. He'd seemed so responsible, earnest, and hardworking.

Turns out he was simply a great actor.

But that wasn't where her mind needed to be right now, so she reined it in. "Let's see if we can get some answers."

The pair exited the cruiser, and she activated the pen camera in her pocket as they approached the front door. Rebecca rapped firmly on the polished wood, and within moments, the door swung open to reveal Jay Griles. He was wearing a polo shirt with the collar popped like a frat boy from the eighties. Tattoos swirled down both arms and even showed at the unbuttoned neck.

He pulled back in surprise and terror on seeing them, clutching a backpack as if it were a lifeline. Behind him, a duffel bag and several stacks of clothing were piled up on the floor. They'd clearly interrupted him in the middle of running away like a scared child.

Rebecca noted his haggard appearance. "Going somewhere?"

"None of your business." Griles managed to recover swiftly, tucking his backpack behind his legs.

"We had an incident last night at the station. Someone with a neck tattoo broke in. You wouldn't happen to have one yourself, would you?"

Jay's hand shot up to his collar, yanking it higher around his neck. "No. Now leave me alone." His gaze shifted to Trent, a challenge flickering in his eyes. "If you know what's good for you, you'll leave too."

"Is that a threat?" Rebecca kept her voice cool and steady. "Are you threatening my deputy?"

"No. Look, I'm busy." Griles started backing away, frustration bleeding into his words. "I have to go."

"Are you afraid the Sawyers are after you?" Trent's question hung in the air like an axe poised to fall.

Griles froze, his face a mask of poorly feigned confusion. "The Sawyers? Who...who are they?" He was wide-eyed, the lie shining through loud and clear.

"Cut the crap, Griles. We can protect you if you cooperate." Rebecca's voice was firm, unwavering. "Did the Sawyers force you into helping them last night? Maybe we have a common enemy."

"Protect me?" Griles laughed bitterly, his fear momentarily replaced by anger. "You couldn't even protect your own sheriff's station. I'm getting the hell off this island. So unless you have a warrant for my arrest, I'm out of here."

With that, he slammed the door in their faces, leaving them standing on the doorstep with nothing but questions. Rebecca turned off the pen camera and clenched her fists. She could practically taste the truth, tantalizingly close yet still out of reach.

"Let's go."

Trent and Rebecca strode through the manicured lawn. The salty breeze from Oyster Bay tugged at their clothes, as if urging them to reconsider their path.

Something had changed, and whatever it was, it had Griles running scared. Rebecca knew she'd have to dig deeper if she wanted answers. They were close, and she would not let Griles or the other two men who'd destroyed her station slip through her fingers.

"Something's off." Trent's dark eyes narrowed as he swiveled his head to look around them.

"Tell me about it." Rebecca's own frustration bubbled under the surface. Still, it was reassuring to see Trent acting with such professionalism. He'd promised not to fuck up, and so far, he hadn't. "He was scared, really scared. And that lie about the Sawyers? He's hiding something."

"Plus, did you see him shift his collar up tight on his neck?" Trent rubbed his clean-shaven jawline. "If he's innocent, wouldn't he want to prove it?"

"Exactly." Rebecca's mind raced as she considered the possibilities. "I think you were right. He must've been one of the guys who broke into the station. Which begs the question, why would he be leaving in such a rush? If he did what the Sawyers wanted, they should have his back."

"If that's what happened, then we're missing something." Trent opened the passenger door and got in, his bruised face at odds with the sharp mind beneath. "Maybe he planned to do one last job and then bail, thinking they'd spare him."

"Like a *get out of jail free* card?" Rebecca smirked as she crossed the front of the SUV and climbed in. As she settled in her seat next to Trent, her eyes never left the waterfront mansion. "He's got money, and he's obviously trying to get away from here as fast as possible. Something must've happened since last night that he didn't expect."

"Could be he thought the Sawyers would allow him to flee after doing the break-in for them, but they changed their minds. That would explain his panic and sudden need to escape."

"Possibly." Rebecca tore her gaze away from the house. "But we still don't have any solid proof. We need something more concrete."

"Hey." A glint of inspiration shined in Trent's eyes. "What about checking out Mystic Visions Tattoo Studio? It's the only tattoo parlor on the island, and I've heard some of the Aqua Mafia guys got their ink done there. Maybe they can show us Griles's tattoo."

"Good idea." That was an easy way to get around the guy's

refusal to show off his ink. The lead might be a long shot, but it was worth exploring. "Let's go check it out."

The cruiser pulled away, leaving behind the sprawling estate and its panicked occupant fearfully watching them from the window. Somehow, Rebecca didn't think it was them Jay Griles was really afraid of.

11

The smell of antiseptic mingled with the earthy scents of incense and tattoo ink as Rebecca and Trent entered Mystic Visions Tattoo Parlor. A petite blond woman with full-sleeve tattoos on both arms looked up from behind the front desk.

"Hi, there. I'm Lisa. What can I do for you today?"

Rebecca tapped the badge on her belt. "I'm Sheriff Rebecca West and this is Deputy Trent Locke. We need to speak to any tattoo artists that work here."

"That's only Todd Feldman. This is his shop. I do the piercings." Lisa nodded at a curtain that hid a section of the building. The buzz of a tattoo gun came from behind it. "He's just finishing up with a client. Should be maybe ten more minutes if you want to have a seat."

Rebecca glanced around the waiting area adorned with framed tattoo designs while Trent wandered over to examine the tattoo aftercare products. His idea of coming down to ask about the tattoo seemed to be a good one. There were photos of all kinds of pieces on different body parts displayed on all the walls.

"So do you get a lot of tourists coming in for tattoos?"

"Oh yeah, tons." Lisa sighed and dropped her chin in her hand, leaning forward on the desk. "Mostly, they go for the small souvenir kind of pieces, lighthouses, seashells, Old Witch's Cottage. Todd prefers working on the bigger, more artistic stuff, but we can't say no to the tourism dollars. If I had a dime for every basic girl asking for a dolphin or sea turtle tattoo with waves in the background, I'd be rich."

Rebecca chuckled as she freed her phone from her pocket and signed into her work account. "Ever seen this guy before? Name's Jay Griles." She held up Jay Griles's driver's license photo.

Lisa peered at the screen, scrunching her nose around a stud in thought. "Looks kind of familiar, but I can't place him."

"Thanks anyway." Rebecca tucked the phone back into her pocket. She and Trent took a seat, idly flipping through tattoo design books as they waited.

Twenty minutes later, the hanging curtain opened, and out walked a sweet-looking elderly lady admiring the fresh ink on her wrist, tightly wrapped in plastic. "Looks amazing, dear. Thank you so much!"

Todd Feldman emerged, wiping his hands on a cloth. His buzz-cut hair and glasses gave him a serious demeanor, contrasted by the impressive array of tattoos covering his arms. "No problem, Mrs. Jersey. You take good care of it, and I'll see you in a few weeks for your next session." Todd's gaze darted to Rebecca, then back to Lisa. "Can you handle that while I get cleaned up?"

After Mrs. Jersey paid and left, Todd turned to Rebecca and Trent, clearly intrigued by the pair of officers in his parlor. "Hey, guys. What can I do for you?"

Rebecca made the introductions. "Someone with a tattoo broke into the station. We're trying to identify him. You recognize this guy?" She showed Todd the photo of Griles.

"Ah, that Yacht Club motherfucker." Todd's face showed a mixture of recognition and disgust.

Clearly, Trent had been right. Griles was an asshole.

"I remember working on his back and neck piece."

"Can you describe it?" Trent's eyes narrowed in anticipation.

"Uh…it was a while ago, so my memory's fuzzy. But I take photos of all my pieces and archive them. Give me a sec." Todd disappeared into a back room, leaving Rebecca and Trent to exchange impatient glances. They could hear him shuffling things around, muttering to himself.

Rebecca called out, raising her voice just enough to be heard. "What was your experience like with Griles and his Aqua Mafia friends?"

"Shitty bunch of people." There was no hesitation in Todd's voice. "Some of my most lucrative clients, but Griles was a total jerk, making jokes about how he'd have to come back for touch-ups because the girls he's with would scratch up his back."

Trent gave her a look, agreeing with Todd.

"Got it!" Todd reappeared, holding a photograph of an expansive black tattoo covering Griles's back and neck. His head was turned, showing his profile in the picture.

"It was some kind of weird tribal symbol he wanted supersized on his back. He thought it would link his shoulder pieces he got done somewhere else, but they're a different style, so it looks like crap."

"Boss, that's the same tattoo as the guy from the station."

Rebecca agreed. The unique shape and shading of the tattoo were unmistakable.

"Thanks, Todd. This helps more than you know."

"Anything I can do to help get rid of those dickheads." He passed over the picture. "I've got more, so you can take this one for evidence if you need it."

Trent reached out and took it. "Thanks, man. Think you got any more of the members among your collection?"

Todd and Lisa shared a look. "I'm sure we do. They tend to come around here in packs. Flashing money, not tipping, and acting like big shots. One thing I got to give them, though, they never flinch under the needle."

Rebecca thought about the permanent marker she'd seen on Mary Bergman, a young woman who was murdered for trying to escape the Yacht Club. "Have you ever tattooed the words *pain slut* on a young woman's thigh?"

Todd's face dropped, and Lisa made a scoffing noise. Or maybe it was a gagging noise. "No. Never. Never been asked." He shook his head. "I'm not shaming anyone with that kink, but it's not something I'd be comfortable putting permanently on someone's skin."

It had been worth a shot. If Todd had done that tattoo, Rebecca might've been able to track down more of the Aqua Mafia victims. "It was just a hunch. Again, thanks for this."

As they left the tattoo parlor, Rebecca was satisfied with what they had. They'd found the evidence they needed to place Griles at that station, and now they were one step closer to bringing down the criminals who plagued their small town. One by one, she would knock them off their pedestals.

A wisp of fog drifted past Rebecca's face as she and Trent stood outside the tattoo parlor, silently comparing the parlor's photo to the one from the surveillance footage. The trailing point of the intricate tribal symbol that reached up to Jay Griles's neck was a perfect match to the man they'd seen in the video.

"Looks like we've got him." Rebecca tucked her phone into her pocket and glanced over at Trent, who'd been unusually quiet since they left the shop. His eyes were narrowed, and a crease had formed between his eyebrows.

"Are we really going to arrest him? Just like that?" Trent asked, his voice low and uncertain.

"Yep." Rebecca tried to keep her own uncertainty from showing. "We've got him identified committing a felony, so we don't need to wait for a judge. And besides, it's better this way. No paper trail to warn the bastard about what we're doing."

12

I stared at the phone in my hand as I reclined in my armchair, the black leather creaking beneath me. There was nothing to see outside except gray on gray as the second day of rain continued. The screen lit up, and I was giddy as Archer's name flashed across it.

"Tell me you have good news," I purred into the phone, well aware of the effects it had on my new man.

"Jay won't get far." Archer's deep voice oozed with sexy confidence. "I staked out his place an hour ago, and I've been watching him ever since. He's packing, like you expected. Then he had a visit from the sheriff and that punching bag of a deputy. He didn't talk long, but I think Jay's outlived his usefulness."

"That's what I like to hear." I smiled, satisfied. Jay was always going to die, since I couldn't risk him escaping with all that he knew. But after learning that Ryker had been talking to the police, I'd moved up the timeline on Luka's death to serve as a warning to everyone else. "Are you sure you can make the shot you need?"

"With one hand tied behind my back." Archer's self-assurance sent tingles up my thighs. "You said he'd never leave his beloved boat behind. I'm waiting near the inlet that connects Oyster Bay to the open ocean. Considering how fast he's packing, I'm certain he'll be here soon."

Archer's eagerness to please me was intoxicating. A powerful, muscular, younger man who was more than willing to do my bidding.

Jim would never dirty his hands like this. As fun as my husband could be, in bed and out of it, he never killed his victims. In the past, that had been enough for me. Together, we'd take months, sometimes years, to break and refashion our playthings. They'd cry and scream so prettily under our hands.

By the time we finished training them, our little pets would beg for more pain, eager to do anything I asked. I loved having those sweet, delicate creatures under my control. But having a big, strong man under my power? I shivered uncontrollably. This was proving to be so much more satisfying.

My mind wandered to what else I could make Archer do once our current problem was resolved. A man like him could be useful in many ways. "I hope your aim is still as sharp as ever," I teased, goading him. How much would he endure for me? "Will you be able to hit Griles while he's on his boat?"

"Ex-military, remember?" Archer's tone was confident but left no room for further questions about his past. Of course, if she wanted to know, she would. She was certain she could get him to do anything, share everything.

"Of course. How could I forget?" I laughed.

"Tell me something. You're such a strong, amazing, straightforward woman. What went wrong with Ryker? How did he turn out so weak?"

Archer's question dampened my lusty thoughts. I

considered how to respond. "Ryker has his moments of usefulness, but you're right, he's weak." I pushed back, sensing an opportunity. "And what about your mother, Archer? Did she make you the man you are today?"

Archer didn't take the bait, instead deflecting the question. "I wouldn't credit her with anything. She wasn't even a sliver of the woman you are. Which is why I'm so confused by Ryker having grown into what he is when he had a role model like you."

I'd struck a nerve. This man had mommy issues, and I could use that. Already, he was an expert at praising and pleasing me. Maybe he would become my new pet, filling the void left by the empty kennels after all my bitches had to be put down. I missed the delicate little girls who knew when to heel, when to sit, and when to please their masters.

"I'm in position." Archer's voice tore me from my fantasy.

"Very good." I leaned back in my chair, the phone cradled against my ear. I scanned the vast grayness outside the window as my imagination took over. Griles on his boat, desperately trying to escape the island. I smiled.

"Archer." I wanted him to know what I was feeling. "I want you to keep me on the line when you take the shot. I want to hear it."

"Of course." A hint of excitement laced his words. "But we have some time before he shows up."

"Good," I purred. "Tell me exactly what you're going to do to him."

Archer took a deep breath, as if readying himself for a performance. "Once I see him on his boat, I'll wait for the perfect moment and pull the trigger. The bullet will tear through his chest. The red stain will spread across his shirt like ink on wet parchment. His body will collapse under his weight. Jay will die alone, on the boat he treasured so much, moments from the freedom he seeks."

I closed my eyes, losing myself in the imagery. I could practically see Jay's face contorting in pain and surprise as he clutched at his wound. The confusion in his eyes as he tried to figure out who killed him and why.

"Then what?" I whispered, my heart racing.

"Once he's dead, I'll board the boat, taking control of it." Archer's enthusiasm seemed to match my own, and it left me nearly breathless. "I'll cut out his eyes, as you requested. He won't ever witness anything again, not even in death."

My breath caught in my throat as my fingers trailed down my neck to my chest. "Ah, yes. That's perfect. Go on."

"Are you...enjoying this?" Archer asked, genuine curiosity in his voice.

"More than you know." I breathed into the receiver of the phone, reveling in the illicit thrill of our conversation.

"That's so hot." He chuckled, his confidence seeming to increase with my growing lust. "I want you to enjoy this as much as I will."

"Trust me, I plan too." I slid my hand inside my silk blouse, glad I hadn't bothered to put a bra on after my shower.

My thoughts turned to the message I sent that morning, warning the island's residents not to interfere with my plans. Jay Griles's death would serve as a powerful reminder of the consequences for disobedience. They'd think twice about crossing me now. And if any of them didn't do as they were told, I could enjoy another moment like this.

"Archer." I snapped out of my thoughts, seized by an irresistible urge to share my excitement with my new plaything. "Do you realize what a strong message this will send? Killed while trying to escape the island? They'll be too terrified to cross me after this."

"Exactly. No one will dare stand in your way."

"Don't forget to make sure Griles's laptop falls into the correct hands. Remember this is just step one."

"Step one of eliminating anyone who opposes you."

Elimination. The word buzzed through me.

"Your lethal loyalty is...heady." My tone was lusty, conveying my appreciation and desire.

"Anything for you." I could almost hear the smile on his lips.

It had been a long time since I'd felt this alive. The thrill of the hunt coursed through my veins, the anticipation of Jay's demise fueling my fire. Knowing that Archer was so eager to carry out my wishes only deepened the exhilaration.

"Keep your eyes open, Archer." I could barely contain my excitement. "I don't want Griles to slip away."

"Understood. He won't leave this island alive."

"Good," I whispered. "Tell me when you pull the trigger. I want to go at the same time."

13

Hands trembling, Jay stuffed his laptop and other essentials inside his duffel bag and zipped it up. Sweat trickled down his forehead, an indication of the fear that constricted his chest like a vise. He'd been a fool to agree to help break into the station last night.

The moment he'd found out Gilroy and Vale were dead, his world turned upside down. Murdered in cold blood. That idiot Luka was behind it, but no one knew why. The Sawyers must have put him up to it. They were always pulling strings from the shadows, and they'd gotten worse recently.

That was when he should've left. Staying put and risking arrest during the break-in as a last-ditch effort to maintain his standing in the Yacht Club had sealed his fate.

"Dammit." Jay glanced around his disheveled living room. His heart raced as he considered the few Yacht Club members who knew the Sawyers were in charge. As far as he knew, he was the last member alive with that knowledge. Which could put a bounty on his head. He needed to leave, and he needed to do it fast.

When the Sawyers asked for his help, Jay had naively

believed he could earn their favor and avoid meeting the same fate as Gilroy and Vale. But that plan shattered into pieces when Archer hacked Luka's hand off without hesitation as the man clung to life.

Everyone knew Vera liked to keep trophies from her enemies. She was sending a message, and he'd received it loud and clear. Time to get out of Dodge.

He studied his belongings, debating what he should bring. It seemed foolish to ponder whether to pack his Ermenegildo Zegna tailored suit or if he should bring his Hermès belt with its distinctive H buckle instead, but the Saint Laurent leather biker jacket was a no-brainer. He'd make room for that staple of his wardrobe.

Shoving a few more items into his bag, he tried to remember if he'd gassed up his boat after his last outing. After all, he'd known for a long while the boat would be his means of escape. He smiled, thinking of the last girl he'd boned on the deck. She'd said she was sixteen, but her body turned him on in ways only an older woman could. He'd stayed out for three days with her before returning.

Shaking thoughts of happier times from his mind, he zipped the bag to close it, pushing in the contents to force everything to fit. Once he was away from Vera and Jim, he could trawl for new girls to pass the time with. Right now, he needed to focus.

With the club falling apart thanks to that new sheriff, Vera and Jim cleaning house made sense.

Anyone with dirt on them was at risk. The Sawyers had assured people from the beginning that they had an in with the sheriff and that she wouldn't bother them. They'd been wrong.

When the lady sheriff had found Bryson Gilroy's killer so fast, Jay had even believed she was on the payroll. After all, buying a cop was cheap and useful. But that was an ongoing expense, while buying an assassin was one and done.

"Maybe I can find someone to take them out." He clenched his fists as he stared at the possessions he was abandoning. "If I hire a killer, it won't matter if they have an assassin. An assassin who can't get paid will simply disappear. And with the vacancies at the top of the food chain, I can come back and take over."

Luka's obedience had been rewarded with him losing his hand and his life. That message confirmed Jay's suspicions. His time was up. And with the sheriff hot on his heels after recognizing his tattoo, the walls were closing in on him. Leaving was his only option.

"Jesus, what a mess." Slinging the duffel bag over his shoulder, he cast one last desperate look around the room before heading to the door, heart pounding in his ears.

"Keep your shit together. You just need to get out of here."

As Jay crept through the shadows of his own home, every creak and groan of the floorboards sounded like mini explosions giving away his location. The once-familiar space now felt like a labyrinth designed to trap him, with unseen eyes watching his every move. His breath hitched as he stepped into the cold, wet air, nerves frayed and senses on high alert.

Watch your back. He sprinted across his yard toward the pier. The misting rain had already soaked him to the bone, but he ignored that slight discomfort. *One wrong move and you're done for.*

Jay's pulse quickened with every step, his mind racing with thoughts of the Sawyers' wrath and the sheriff's pursuit. Right when he'd been getting on the good side of Vera and Jim, everything had spiraled out of control. But as he neared the boat that would carry him to freedom, a glimmer of hope sparked within him. If he could make it to the open ocean, he might stand a chance at survival.

Wind whispered through the tall grass lining the pier as Jay made his way toward his ticket to freedom. His heart pounded in his ears, drowning out the sound of the waves lapping against the shoreline. Shadows cast by passing clouds danced around him, morphing into imagined pursuers with every step. The weight of the laptop and the secrets it contained seemed to grow heavier with each passing second.

"Almost there," he mumbled, clenching his teeth as he fought to maintain control of his frayed nerves.

As he reached the boat, a sense of relief washed over him, momentarily drowning out his paranoia. He stepped onto the vessel, bags in tow, and silently prayed his plan would work. Glancing at the island that had once been his sanctuary, Jay couldn't help but feel a twinge of sadness amidst the fear that gripped him. Tossing the mooring ropes on the dock, he gave his house a farewell look.

But there was no time for sentimentality. He needed to get far away before the Sawyers or the sheriff caught up to him.

Some of his anxiety left him as he noted the fuel tank was more than three-quarters full. He fired up the engine and steered the vessel away from the pier. The salty sea breeze stung his face, a harsh reminder of the unforgiving world he was leaving behind. Water stretched before him, dark and infinite, offering both salvation and peril. The idle speed he needed to maintain to not draw unwanted attention from his neighbors made the short distance feel interminable.

With each passing moment, Jay's heartbeat slowed, his fear gradually giving way to a newfound determination. He would escape the Sawyers' clutches and the relentless sheriff or die trying. A glimmer of hope flickered within his chest.

"Once I'm free, I'll find someone who can take care of the Sawyers." He gripped the steering wheel.

The boat cut through the water slowly as the inlet drew closer with each agonizing second. He could almost taste the freedom that lay just beyond it, a world where he was no longer a pawn in someone else's game.

As he neared the inlet and the promise of escape it held, a sudden, brutal force slammed into his chest, nearly toppling him over. Searing agony tore through him, forcing the breath from his lungs.

Was he having a heart attack? He looked down to find blood spreading across his shirt.

What the hell?

His thoughts raced, grappling with the reality of his situation even as his vision began to swim. Legs buckling beneath him, he stumbled, colliding with the steering wheel. As desperation fueled his final moments, the boat veered off course, careening toward the unforgiving shoreline.

He choked, fighting against the darkness that threatened to claim him.

As the boat ran aground on the rocky shore, Jay Griles took his last breath, his secrets and regrets dying with him.

14

The radio crackled to life, interrupting Rebecca's drive back to Jay Griles's house. Hoyt's voice came through, urgent and strained. "Boss, we've got a situation here. A civilian called in a beached boat on the north side of Oyster Bay. We ran the name, and it belongs to Griles. He's got a home in the same area too. Darby and I are almost there."

An annoyed groan escaped Rebecca's lips before she could stop it. This was too much of a coincidence to ignore. She exchanged a brief glance with Trent, who looked as pissed off as she was.

"We're on our way."

She turned onto the road leading up around the bay instead of the one that would take her to Griles's house. The road narrowed as houses gave way to foliage, all stained with the reds and browns of fall. She slowed as the road narrowed again, dropping from paved lanes to gravel, and followed it all the way to the rocky beach by the inlet.

Rebecca climbed out of the cruiser and took in the tableau before her, Trent hustling to join her. Hoyt, Greg, Jake, and Viviane were already on-site. And there, in the midst of it all, lay the boat belonging to Jay Griles. It had beached on the rocks, waves lapping at its hull.

The salt-laden air stung Rebecca's nostrils as she approached the beached boat, its hull scarred by the jagged rocks that had brought it to a sudden halt.

"Darby!"

The deputy looked up from her camera, her dark eyes attentive. "Boss!" Viviane hopped off the boat onto the rocky shore.

Hoyt called out to them without preamble, his tight lips revealing the gravity of the situation. "Griles is dead. Single shot to the chest, probably pierced his heart. His eyes have been cut out too."

"Three makes it a signature. Moore's tongue, Reynold's hand, and Griles's eyes. That lines up with the idea of this being an assassin. They're sometimes required to show proof of death to get paid."

"Yeah, this one is oddly…" Viviane trailed off, wrinkling her nose. "Clean? There's barely any blood. It's like he just plucked them out. Can you do that? Just pluck an eye out without cutting things up? It's creepy looking." She shuddered. "Well, maybe it was done postmortem. At least, I hope it was. That would produce less blood."

"It's called enucleation. And it's not as easy as plucking an eye out." As they approached the grounded boat, Rebecca winced at the sight of the man's lifeless body and his empty sockets. She clenched her jaw, fighting the anger that threatened to rise in her throat. This wasn't what she'd wanted. Griles deserved justice, not this.

If he'd only listened to us a few hours ago and accepted our protection, he'd still be alive.

"Nobody saw him get shot. I guess no one was keeping an eye out for him." Hoyt grinned and bounced his eyebrows a few times while Viviane groaned at his pun.

Rebecca shook her head. "That was a bad one, Frost. Can you try and keep your eye on the ball here, instead of cracking jokes?"

"Yeah, Frost. That one was so thin it was barely visible." Viviane grinned proudly while Hoyt gave her a nod of approval. Their squeamish rookie was catching on to using humor to diffuse the horror of their jobs.

Rebecca waved for her senior deputy to continue with his report.

Hoyt checked his notes. "Some people came out when they saw the boat on the rocks. No one seems to have seen anything. This area is a no-wake zone, and the boat couldn't have been going more than five miles per hour. Probably didn't want to draw attention to himself either. The boat basically slid up on the rocks. I doubt there was much to hear."

Abner and Coffey took witness statements, their faces a mix of concentration and disbelief. Rebecca got the idea that whoever had killed Griles had known exactly what they were doing and how to cover their tracks.

"Who could've done this?" Her voice was barely audible over the waves slapping against the hollow hull.

"Someone who knew his plans or knew him well enough to know he'd run." Trent's words echoed her own thoughts. "We need to find out how that person fits into all this. We were about to arrest Griles when we got the call."

"Looks like someone beat us to the punch." Viviane held up a small evidence bag containing the crumpled remains of a bullet. "Found this lodged in the boat's hull. Judging by the weight and shape, I'd say it's a rifle round. Sniper shot, most likely. Did you see anyone near his house earlier?"

"Nobody who stood out." Rebecca's mind replayed the moments leading up to their discovery as Viviane gestured toward where the witnesses were standing and giving statements. "Why?"

"Seems odd, doesn't it?" Viviane mused. "Someone must've known he was leaving, like Trent just said. Otherwise, why bother with a sniper rifle? They couldn't just assume he'd be out on his boat."

Rebecca's stomach tightened with unease. That meant someone knew his character well enough to anticipate his flight. A traitor within their midst, perhaps? Or an accomplice turned executioner?

"Keep processing the scene. Trent and I are going back to his place. Maybe there's more evidence to be found."

"Sure thing, Boss." Viviane's camera was already clicking away as she resumed her work.

As Rebecca and Trent made their way toward the cruiser, she tried not to think about Ryker. The Yacht Club was more than willing to kill their own members instead of risking the police getting their hands on them. Had they freed him from jail solely to kill him later? Or would his standing as the son of the leaders be enough to keep him safe?

As they drove away from the crime scene, Rebecca couldn't shake the eerie feeling that the eyes of an unseen predator were watching their every move.

15

Trent slumped against the cool leather of the passenger seat, glancing out at the trees as Rebecca steered the cruiser once more toward Jay Griles's home. His heart skipped a beat as they pulled up to see the front door hanging wide open. He exchanged a worried glance with Rebecca.

"Someone's been here." She grabbed the radio and called in to let the others know what they'd found and to put them on standby. With a glance toward him, she reached down and unsnapped her gun holster before she got out. "Stay alert."

Trent followed her lead. They approached the house cautiously, guns drawn but pointed at the ground.

He stepped wide around Rebecca as she tucked close against the frame of the door and peered in.

Inside, the place looked untouched. What had someone come here looking for?

Did they find it?

Moving single file, they made their entrance, clearing the first room. Rebecca gave him a nod, indicating they should cover the whole house. Following her lead, they cleared room after room. He was relieved when he didn't screw up even once.

Trent called on the radio, letting the others know the house was clear for forensics to come over. Rebecca had gone to check the back door that led to the dock while Trent searched the front room.

A laptop sat open on a coffee table among the chaos. Donning a pair of gloves, Trent rubbed the touch pad. The screen sprang to life, revealing an email that appeared to be encrypted. "I found something," he called out.

A moment later, Rebecca's footsteps alerted him as she made her way back to the front room.

"Seems like our friend Jay here left his laptop unlocked." It would've been a hassle to get a warrant for the device, but since it was unlocked and had programs opened, they didn't need to worry about that. He clicked the email icon on the taskbar, showing it was open and signed in as well.

A sharp breath came from Rebecca at his back. "Good find. What's it say?"

He paraphrased the email out loud. "He was reading an email from BC1 that he got a couple hours ago. It says there's a meeting tonight, with time and coordinates to be provided later. A boat will be waiting for everyone to meet up."

"That's it?"

"Yep."

"Things are moving fast." Rebecca stepped up beside him and read the rest of the email. She frowned. "We need a game plan."

"Looks like we've got ourselves a piece of evidence." Trent tried and failed to mask his excitement. "Maybe we can finally catch these bastards."

Rebecca's eyes narrowed as she looked at her phone. "Let's hope so. We don't have a warrant, but we don't need to leave this for anyone else either. Go ahead and bag it and tag it. Then slide it under the couch. Once we get the warrant, we can come back for it."

"Good idea."

Trent ran out to the cruiser to get an evidence bag from the cargo space. On his way, he noticed a doorbell camera on the house across the street. Carrying the items he'd need, Trent returned to where Rebecca was taking pictures.

"Boss, let's pay a visit to the neighbor across the street. I saw a doorbell camera. Maybe it caught something that would be useful."

"Can't hurt to try." Rebecca headed outside.

Trent finished filling out the label on the bag, dropped the laptop inside, and slid it under the couch as Rebecca had instructed. Stuffing his gloves into his pocket, he hurried across the street, eager to catch up.

He reached her as she knocked on the door. A moment later, it creaked open to reveal an elderly man with gray hair and a heavyset build. He peered at them through thick glasses, curiosity in his eyes. "Can I help you?"

"Yes, sir. I'm Deputy Trent Locke, and this is Sheriff Rebecca West." Trent pointed to himself and then his boss.

The man nodded. "I'm Rick Leonard." He held out his hand to shake.

Trent reached out, careful not to squeeze too hard. "We're investigating the murder of your neighbor, Jay Griles.

"Murder?" Mr. Leonard scratched his temple, surprise slackening his jaw. "I was sure I'd seen him out today. Earlier. Looked fine."

"Mind if we take a look at your doorbell camera footage from today?"

"Uh, sure." Mr. Leonard stepped aside to stare at the doorbell as he dug in his pocket and pulled out his phone. "Just need help figuring out how to work this app for it. Everything's on apps now."

As they huddled around Mr. Leonard's smartphone, Trent sensed the time ticking away. They needed answers, and they needed them fast.

"Here." Rebecca's fingers flew across the screen. "This is the footage from today."

After scrolling past the footage that showed Rebecca stopping by earlier and Jay leaving, she slowed the video. Huddling around the screen, the three of them watched intently as a black car pulled up, its license plate hidden from view due to the angle.

A bald, muscular man stepped out and simply kicked open Griles's front door. He emerged minutes later, apparently empty-handed. The time stamp indicated this had occurred less than an hour after they'd interrupted Jay's packing. Trent pointed to the time and Rebecca nodded.

They had the same man at three different crime scenes. Things were indeed moving fast. And the speed at which things were progressing had Trent's stomach in knots. They thanked Rick Leonard for his assistance and headed back to the cruiser.

As soon as they got in, Rebecca gripped the wheel, apparently deep in thought.

"Boss?"

"We need to put out a BOLO for anyone matching the description of our muscular, bald dude. Also alert the others where we're going and make sure they keep their wits about them. Let's confront the people calling the shots, shall we? It's time we pay the Sawyers a visit."

They rode in silence as Rebecca steered them to their destination. The two-story house was nothing special and a little gaudy to Trent's taste. Its sunny yellow stucco and mint-green trim shouted *ocean view*, though from where he sat, that view was only a sliver of blue. The massive oak tree shading much of the front yard was pretty, though, and

he wondered how many times Ryker had climbed it as
a kid.

Or had he even been allowed to do such basic things?

"Wow." Rebecca frowned at the home. "That's…bright."

Trent chuckled. "Tell me you live on an island without
telling me you live on an island."

She parked the cruiser, and they both stepped out. He
brushed past several tall hedges bordering the sidewalk.

Rebecca joined him as he approached the front door.
Trent couldn't help but admire the intricate wood carvings
adorning it.

"Fancy door for such a simple home, huh?"

She was right. "At least it isn't green."

He reached for the ornate brass knocker and gave it a few
solid raps. When nobody answered, he glanced over at
Rebecca, who shrugged and sidestepped to a window.

Trent did the same on his side of the small porch. No
luck. Thick curtains blocked the view into the house. They
couldn't even take a peek inside. There were no cars in sight.

After knocking one more time, Rebecca sighed.

Trent turned toward her. "Even if they're here, it feels like
they're not going to answer the door."

"Let's go talk to the neighbors. Your idea from Mr.
Leonard's home paid off earlier. And you were right about
visiting the tattoo parlor. Let's see if you can go three for
three."

They'd barely gotten back to the cruiser when Trent
noticed a familiar face. "That's Felicity Pine across the street.
She's the local door-to-door knife saleslady."

"Did we just fall through a 1985 portal or is 'door-to-
door' slang for something?"

Trent laughed. "No, really. Rumor is, she started the job
simply so she could get invited into more people's homes and
sit around and gossip." He pointed to a woman with brown

hair and glasses who was pretending to tend to her garden while staring at them.

"A nosy neighbor. Law enforcement's best friend." Rebecca smiled as she turned into her driveway.

Felicity Pine braced a hand against her knee and stood as they parked and got out.

"Excuse me, Ms. Pine?" Rebecca pointed to her badge. "I'm Sheriff Rebecca West, and this is Deputy Trent Locke. We're looking into the whereabouts of the Sawyers. Have you seen them recently?"

"Oh, hey, Trent. Nice shiner. Ouch."

"Hi, Felicity. Job hazard. How are you?"

"Peachy. The people that live across the street, Sheriff?" Felicity wiped the sweat off her brow and squinted at them. "Not in a few days, no. They tend to keep to themselves. I don't see them often."

"Have you noticed any muscular men around here lately? Around six-three or so?" Trent held his hand up at that height, remembering the man's intimidating presence at the station.

"Muscular? No, nobody like that." Felicity frowned. "Is everything all right?"

"Routine investigation." Rebecca responded before Trent could. "We're asking around, hoping someone has seen him. Thank you for your help."

As they walked back to the cruiser through a light drizzle, Trent tried to make sense of the nagging feeling in his gut. He was doing his best to do everything by the book, but something felt off about Rebecca's interaction with the Sawyers' neighbor.

Why hadn't Rebecca told Felicity the real reason they'd driven out there? Was Rebecca trying to protect them because they were Ryker's folks? Trent briefly pondered that before the answer struck him. She didn't want Felicity to know they'd been looking for the Sawyers because she didn't want to give them a heads-up if they happened to talk to their neighbor. She withheld information for the integrity of the investigation.

He was feeling good about their progress and his contributions to the investigation. But an assassin was on the loose, and they didn't know who he might target next.

16

Rebecca paced back and forth in Trent's front room once again. After forensics had shown up and taken over the scene, she'd called a meeting to bring everyone together.

"Tell me what you learned at the scene after we left." Rebecca directed her words at Hoyt, who stood in a shadowed corner. He pointed to Viviane.

She cleared her throat. "All right. I went ahead and investigated a few possible places the sniper could've been hiding, and the most likely option is the grassy area at the opening of the bay. It's around a hundred meters away and has a straight line of sight to Griles's house. We'll need a full forensic report to confirm or rule it out, but the vantage point makes sense, and the techs are there now."

"Good work, Darby." Rebecca was strained with worry. She rubbed the back of her neck, trying to alleviate some of the tension that had settled there. This wasn't a collection of random killings. This was a plan. A big one. And she didn't know what the end goals were.

Or maybe the plan was fairly basic. Kill anyone who

could tie the Sawyers to the Yacht Club. But the specific targets were a mystery.

Rebecca didn't know how many members were left, since even the ones who lived locally traveled often. She hadn't been in town long enough to know if they were snowbirds who disappeared once the weather turned cold only to reappear with spring.

The Yacht Club had already tried to kill her a few times. Would they go after her people too?

"Someone was just lying there, waiting for Griles to bolt like a scared rabbit." Greg, with his silver hair and deeply wrinkled eyes, sat on the couch, his hands clasped together as he shook his head. "Poor fool walked right into it."

"As for Griles…we found his place with the door kicked in and his laptop open. They're killing their own people, and Griles knew he could be next." Rebecca laid out her theory.

"Why him? If he only helped them bust into the station, you'd think he'd be on their good side now." Hoyt shifted his weight, turning to look at Trent. "It takes a lot of balls for someone to blast into our station and do that to one of our own."

"Maybe he screwed up? Or forgot something? Then when he got that email about the 'meeting,' he realized he was getting played." Greg grunted. "Or with the ways these psychos have been acting recently, maybe he just forgot to say excuse me when he burped."

"Maybe the email is a ruse." Trent gave a nod to Greg's theory.

Rebecca agreed. Aside from not knowing when or where the meeting would occur, she had wondered if it was a ruse too. She couldn't very well call Rhonda or the Coast Guard to tell them there was a possible meeting at a time and location unknown. The situation was maddening.

"Or maybe he heard something when he dropped off

Ryker to wherever they took him. Something that made him realize he was the next target." Hoyt jutted his chin at Rebecca. "You heard what Ryker said they did to him when he pissed them off. Their own child. How much worse do you think they treat people who aren't blood?"

"Or Griles read that email and thought they were going to kill everyone at this point. Tie up all the 'loose ends' in the Aqua Mafia." Rebecca didn't like to think about it, but it had to be said. "We know they kill their people when they get caught. Maybe they think we're closer to taking them all down than we really are, and they're planning a full-on massacre. So he figured it was less risky to make a run for it. Clearly, he was wrong."

Hoyt mumbled something that sounded like, "The bastard."

"Cornered rats will do anything they can to keep from getting caught. The truth is, we have no idea how far the Sawyers are willing to go. But we do know they don't flinch at killing their own to make their lives easier." The room fell silent as the gravity of the situation sank in. Rebecca could see the fear and determination in each of their eyes, a volatile mix that fueled their desire to bring the Sawyers down quickly.

"Rebecca's right." Greg spoke up, his gruff voice steady and resolute. "The Commonwealth's Attorney was very grateful to get the recorded confessions I delivered. Maybe the Sawyers found out, and they feel the noose squeezing closed. But if we can infiltrate this so-called meeting before any of the others get there, we might be able to bring down their hired gun and prevent some needless deaths. We only need to find one Aqua Mafia member who's willing to cooperate."

"Protection in exchange for cooperation." Rebecca's gaze fell on the middle distance as she considered the idea. It had worked well in the past with Robert Leigh. She helped him plead his case for insanity, and he'd told her everything he knew about the Yacht Club.

If they got some of the remaining members to turn, they might even be able to call in the FBI to help. "Who do we have a lot of dirt on? Allen Wilson? Christoph Blake? Christian Mallard?"

"Maybe we don't need dirt on someone to get them on our side." Trent's deep voice resonated through the room. "Why should any of them stay loyal to the Sawyers? Maybe we should find someone and strike a deal."

"Good point." Rebecca weighed their options. They did have a list of known members, but she didn't have it with her at the moment. As an added safety precaution, she didn't carry the Aqua Mafia files on her phone. And the files wouldn't tell her who was likely to turn their back on the Yacht Club anyway. "Do you have anyone in mind?"

"Christian Mallard," Trent answered without hesitation. "He was part of my old group of friends from back in the day." His lips twisted on the word *friends*, making it clear how he felt about them now.

Hoyt leaned forward, arms crossed. "Is he the one who bullied you and then tried to order you to 'keep the beach clear' as a way to get you to hide a body?"

"Y-yeah." Trent's face flushed. "We used to hang out together when we were kids. I haven't talked to him since the beach incident, but…maybe he'll be willing to help us."

"All right, then." Rebecca reached a decision. "We try Christian Mallard. If he doesn't want to cooperate, we'll move on to the next person. But let's hope he sees the chance to save his own life, and others, as more important than blind loyalty to the Sawyers."

Hoyt nodded along with the rest. "If that doesn't work,

we can always see about getting a state police boat to head out there instead."

"If we do that, we run the risk of them scattering before we get close enough." Rebecca shook her head. "And that's the best option. They could also open fire on us and take off running, never to be seen again. No, we need a way to get to this meeting without anyone noticing us. Which means we need to find a way to approach without raising suspicion. We need someone with inside knowledge."

17

Rebecca and Trent approached the door of Christian Mallard's residence, a lavish beachfront property. The last of the daylight had leaked from the sky, and with each rap of knuckles against wood, her nerves twisted tighter.

The door creaked open to reveal a pale, trembling Mallard. "I don't talk to the cops without my lawyer present." He spit the words out before they could even introduce themselves.

"You sure about that?" Rebecca projected a steady and authoritative tone. "Braden Moore is dead. So you'd have to find a lawyer who the Sawyers don't know about, bring them in on the down-low, and hope they don't end up dead too."

Mallard swallowed hard, his gaze darting back and forth between Rebecca and Trent. His Adam's apple bobbed, revealing his nervousness.

"You didn't hear about that?" Trent scoffed. "I guess you've been holed up here, keeping your head down 'til things settle. The problem with that is, you miss what's really happening." Trent pushed the door open with his knuckles, but Mallard stopped it from opening with a foot.

"What do you want?"

"Believe it or not," Trent dropped the hard cop voice, "I want to see you survive this. I don't think most of your friends will. And I think you're the only one who might listen to me."

"Why should I listen to you when you've already proved how disloyal you are?" Mallard shot back. "Friends? Why do you care so much about me or my 'friends'?"

"Did you receive an email this morning?" Rebecca jumped in, not wanting the men to get distracted by their old disputes.

Mallard snapped his jaw shut and glared at Trent. "I don't know what you're talking about."

"Well, I just read it from a dead man's inbox, so let me jog your memory." Rebecca recited the contents of the email.

Mallard's face grew paler with recognition as she spoke, but he still refused to say anything.

"Now," she continued, "what do you think's going to happen at that meeting tonight?"

"I…" Mallard's voice cracked, his fear palpable. "I don't know. I wasn't invited to any such meeting."

Trent slammed his fist against the door and leaned forward, looming over his old friend. "Get your head out of your ass, Christian. You're being invited to your own funeral. Jim and Vera are tired of hunting you guys down one by one, so they're getting all the little lambs to one indefensible location where you're going to be slaughtered."

Rebecca locked eyes with Mallard, her tone cold and certain. "You know what I think? I think the Sawyers are going to murder you and all the other Aqua Mafia members who know a little too much. Have you thought about leaving the island? Your pal Jay Griles had that idea, and it earned him a bullet through the heart."

Mallard's eyes widened in shock, but there was a glimmer

of pain behind them. "Jay's dead?" He looked at Trent for answers and collapsed a little when the deputy nodded.

"I'm sorry, man. I know he was your little brother's friend. But that's why you paid for your bro to go to college in England. Wasn't it?"

This was all news to Rebecca, so she kept quiet and simply listened.

"You knew the Yacht Club wasn't a safe place. That's why, when your mom died, you sent him away."

"What do you want from me?" This time when he asked, Christian's voice barely registered above a whisper.

"Maybe we can help each other." Rebecca softened her expression. "I want to get on the boat for that meeting without scaring whoever's gunning down Yacht Club members. Let Trent and me ride with you on your boat. When the meeting begins, we'll reveal ourselves and make some arrests. We want to stop the Sawyers and the Yacht Club's reign of terror."

"Look, you have no idea how powerful the Sawyers really are." A note of desperation crept into his voice. "Or what they'll do."

Rebecca maintained eye contact until he started squirming. "Oh, I think I have some idea. We're the ones who have to clean up their victims, hired guns, and coconspirators. They also bombed my workplace last night. I know what they're capable of, and that's exactly why they need to be stopped. We'll board the ship and make a bunch of arrests. Jim and Vera Sawyer will spend the rest of their lives in prison."

Mallard hesitated, clearly torn.

Trent sighed and leaned in. "Think about it, Christian. You help us, and then you can take off to live with your brother in England. You can leave your Aqua Mafia ventures and Shadow Island forever. With the Sawyers behind bars, you won't have to watch your back. It's a win-win."

Mallard's shoulders relaxed ever so slightly. The prospect of an escape route seemed to quench some of the fear in his eyes. Rebecca knew they had him, but it was crucial not to let her guard down.

Mallard took a deep breath. He looked at Rebecca and then at Trent, who stood silently beside her, an immovable presence. Finally, he nodded his agreement. "All right." Mallard straightened, his voice a bit stronger. "But I need you to do something for me first."

"What is it?" Rebecca wasn't about to accept just any request but was willing to listen.

"Leave. I can't risk anyone seeing you two at my door like this. And having your cruiser outside's only going to draw attention. I've got Trent's number. I'll call once you're gone."

Rebecca exchanged a glance with Trent, whose eyes bore into her own as if trying to read her thoughts. He gave a slight nod, telling her to trust Mallard. It wasn't a bad thought on Mallard's part either. They knew Jay Griles had been watched, so he might be under surveillance as well.

With that in mind, she supposed she had to take this offer. "Deal." She squared up against him and leaned forward, getting in his face and dropping her voice.

Mallard jerked his head back in immediate reaction to her suddenly aggressive stance.

"Good. Now yell at us to leave, that you're going to call your lawyer, whatever you want."

Catching on, Mallard put both hands on the door and yelled. "Like I said, contact my lawyer, lady, because I'm not talking! Now get the hell off my property."

Trent moved out of the way as Mallard slammed the door closed. Still thinking about the possibility of being watched by a sniper, Rebecca ripped the elastic from her hair and raked her hands through it as if she were angry. "Locke, let's get back to the cruiser and get out of here."

The ever-present rain of the past few days had begun falling again. Spinning on her heel, Rebecca's damp blond hair swung around her face, and her eyes twitched with annoyance at it. She'd learned long ago that her emotions were generally broadcast across her face. But she also knew that she could manipulate her emotions so people would see what she wanted them to.

Trent fell in behind her as they walked through the drizzle to the cruiser and got in. As soon as she was inside, she pulled off down the road, windshield wipers swiping at the droplets. She didn't know where she was going. She simply needed to get away from there.

Within minutes, Trent's phone rang. He pulled the device out and held it up to her—the screen showed an unknown caller—before he answered.

Rebecca motioned for him to put it on speakerphone.

"Hello. You're on speaker."

"That was a smart thing that the sheriff did. You can think on your feet. We might survive this after all, but we need a plan." Mallard sounded much more composed now.

"Thanks." Rebecca pushed her hair back again. "I do plan on surviving this meeting and saving as many other people as I can. If the Sawyers or their assassin start shooting, we'll take them down."

"How are you planning to do that?"

Rebecca had been thinking about that since she'd first seen the email. "Once everyone at the meeting realizes they were double-crossed, they're not going to fight too hard to save Vera and Jim. Out of sheer self-preservation, they'll turn against the Sawyers."

"So your plan is just to show up, save the day, and wait for them to happily line up to go to jail like good little boys and girls?" Mallard's laugh was brittle.

"Jail? For what?" Rebecca's question stopped him cold. "Being a victim of an assassination attempt isn't a crime. If they don't have any outstanding warrants, we won't even hold them." She scowled.

There was no need to hide her expressions during a phone call. While what she was saying was all technically true, she did plan to get prints, DNA, and photographs of everyone present.

"We'll also give them the opportunity to talk with the Commonwealth's Attorney about any other crimes they might know of Jim, Vera, or Ryker Sawyer committing."

If any of them were linked to the abduction or abuse of children, there'd be no deals. She'd make sure of that.

"The Commonwealth's Attorney?"

"I can reach out to the FBI as well, if you—"

"No!"

Rebecca glanced at Trent, who shrugged. "Why not?"

"Don't…" Mallard sighed. "Don't call the FBI, the state police, or the Coast Guard, okay? Not unless you want the Sawyers to know what you're planning."

The hair rose on Rebecca's arms. "They have plants in each of them?"

"Yes. Powerful plants. You need to keep this small."

Rebecca's mind was whirling, but she instinctually knew that what Mallard said was true. Tonight could only be her and her team. "Okay."

There was a long pause. "Where should I pick you up?"

"Dee's Docks." Rebecca answered without hesitation. Dee was a stand-up guy, the sort of person who wouldn't ask too many questions or share info with the Sawyers. Besides, it was a working dock with most people gone at that time of night. "The water there is deep enough to handle a yacht."

"Fine," Mallard agreed. "But if this goes south, you'd better have a backup plan."

"Let us know if you get another email with time and coordinates. It'd be useful for putting a Plan B together to know exact locations."

But how could she have a damn backup plan if she couldn't trust any of the federal agencies?

Rebecca's heart was pounding at the thought of what they were about to attempt. The last time she'd taken such drastic action, they'd lost Darian. She willed the gut twisting aside, focusing on the task at hand. Rebecca wouldn't allow herself to think about Little Quell.

"Trust me. We'll be prepared."

At her nod, Trent hung up the phone. "Are you sure about this?"

"Of course not. But it's our best shot at stopping the Sawyers and keeping Mallard alive in the process."

Trent's phone pinged, and he tapped on the screen. "It's Christian. Meeting's at ten tonight, and he's provided a screenshot with the coordinates. He'll meet us at Dee's Dock at nine."

That was just a couple hours away. This was happening too fast.

Rebecca took the next turn, heading for Trent's house and the deputies gathered there. "Let's check the coordinates and try to do as much scouting of the location as we can. Then we need to get ready to face down an entire boatful of criminals who don't have much left to lose."

18

A misty fog hung low over the water, and thick clouds hid the moon, pitching the night into darkness. Trent and Rebecca stood side by side on the pier at Dee's Docks. His back was tight with anxiety, same as always when he worked one-on-one with his boss.

Wallace had never been so intimidating.

Trent swallowed, trying not to look nervous as he checked their surroundings one more time. The dock was empty, with the working boats gone for the day and everyone else likely at home.

Viviane, Greg, and Hoyt were already on a boat Greg had borrowed from his friends. And they'd taken off. They were waiting nearby for the signal—that everything was taken care of, or that their help was needed. Tonight was either going to be a near-perfect victory or a total loss. Which was why Rebecca had prepared them for either eventuality.

He and Rebecca were wearing Kevlar vests under their uniforms, and they had one to lend to Mallard as well. The weight of the protective gear was a constant reminder of the danger ahead. They weren't going to risk Mallard getting shot while he helped them. Trent scanned the water, watching as Christian Mallard's yacht glided into view.

"Remember," he turned to Rebecca, who seemed more interested in the island behind them, "this isn't Mallard's party boat. This is the smaller one he uses to cruise along the coast. It's pretty fast, faster than most. In case we need to get away later."

Rebecca nodded, turning to face the approaching yacht. "Got it."

As the yacht neared, Trent caught the line that Christian tossed to him without a word. The same way he'd done when they were younger, he helped pull it closer to the dock.

Memories washed over him of times spent on this very boat, laughing and drinking with friends, feigning interest in fishing when he knew nothing about it. But then his thoughts turned to people he now realized were actual friends.

It had been Greg, his retraining officer, who'd finally shown him how to fish. Greg had taken him out on the water only a few months prior.

On that one day, Trent had caught his first fish. It hadn't been a large one, but it filled him with pride, nonetheless. Greg had even offered to have it mounted as a keepsake, sending it off to a taxidermist.

"Ready?" Rebecca's voice broke through his reverie.

"Ready." His nerves were starting to creep in, now that the hour was approaching.

The first time he'd gone out with the sheriff, the night ended up with Wallace dead. He was determined not to let anyone die this time.

He climbed aboard the yacht, offering a hand to Rebecca as she followed suit. Once they were both on deck, Trent set the mooring line back down near the railing while Mallard adjusted his Kevlar vest under his orange windbreaker. The tension hung heavy in the air. Even Mallard, usually so confident, refused to meet Trent's gaze as he returned to the helm.

As the boat set off, Rebecca and Trent both lost their balance and grabbed onto the closest railing to steady themselves. The bouncing of the boat as it cut through the water was jarring, and the cold ocean water sprayed their faces. Thanks to the low clouds, visibility was limited.

Mallard noticed their struggles. "You'd better come inside. Besides, you might be seen if you stay out there."

They walked inside, crossing the slick deck of the boat and hanging on as they made their way. Inside the bridge cabin, Trent and Rebecca crouched low to avoid detection.

Trent couldn't help but think back to the times spent on this boat with Mallard and how their relationship had changed. But now wasn't the time for reminiscing. Lives were at stake. His focus needed to be razor-sharp.

"Nobody has to die tonight," Trent whispered, his voice barely audible above the hum of the yacht's engine. He fingered the edge of his Kevlar vest, but it brought him no comfort. He couldn't shake the feeling of vulnerability.

"Do you know what kind of boat we'll be meeting on?" Rebecca was looking around the cabin as if taking stock.

Mallard's hand gripped the wheel of the yacht, guiding it skillfully through the choppy waves. The shrouded moon cast an eerie glow over the water as they approached the rendezvous point.

"No idea. I'm just navigating based on the coordinates they provided. You'll see soon enough. We're almost there. Get ready."

Trent took a deep breath and steadied himself, mentally running through the plan one last time. Rebecca met his gaze, steel in her eyes. They were as prepared as they could be, but even the best-laid plans had a way of unraveling when things got messy.

Rebecca started to scramble to reach him but stopped when Hoyt stepped over and knelt next to Darian. Keeping his eyes forward, Hoyt reached down and helped Darian up, then shot the next man to run out. "They got behind us!"

Following Hoyt's example, Rebecca slipped Locke's shotgun sling over his head and hauled him to his feet. "Can you walk?"

"I can run if you can get us out of here." He stared at her holding a shotgun in each hand.

"Then follow me and watch my back." Swinging the shotguns left to right, she sprayed buckshot through the trees. Screams rang out as she pressed forward, Locke limping behind her. Hoyt fell in with her—Darian's arm over his shoulders—as she continued clearing the path to the beach.

The next few moments would determine everything. In the meantime, all they could do was wait and hope luck was on their side.

"Stay down. We're about to come up next to them. The fog won't hide us much longer." Mallard's voice was strained with tension.

Trent and Rebecca exchanged a quick glance, both steeling themselves for the tense moments ahead while they crouched out of sight in the cabin.

"Seems like we're not the only ones who decided to show up early." Mallard nodded toward the boat in the distance. Several other vessels already surrounded it, their hulls bobbing in the dark water so far from shore. A sense of unease hung in the air as they drew closer.

Rebecca rose up to her knees, peering out the window.

Trent was ready to make the call if it looked like their infiltration was compromised. He'd survived the ambush by cartel members on Little Quell Island and never wanted to go through anything like that again.

Rebecca had told him that if he got even a hint of things going wrong, he should say so and bail or call it in. He could see the people on deck now, their body language betraying their confusion and nervousness. They weren't laughing or partying. They seemed tense and subdued. No one was even drinking. Something wasn't right.

"They're scared." Rebecca's head turned as their boat slid up next to the much larger one.

"Stay hidden," Mallard instructed, his eyes locked on the scene unfolding before them. "I'll go see what's going on and keep them distracted."

Trent hesitated, searching his former friend's face for any sign of deception. But all he saw was Mallard's familiar determination, the same loyalty that had once bound them together. With a curt nod, he gave Mallard permission to go ahead.

From their hiding spot, Trent and Rebecca listened as Mallard's voice reached them from the other boat. "Where are the bosses?" His tone was casual but firm.

Murmurs of uncertainty rippled through the group.

"Have you checked the cabins?" Mallard was clearly unwilling to let the matter drop. A few reluctant admissions revealed that no one had bothered, too caught up in their own confusion. As the group began to disperse, Trent knew this was their chance.

"Ready?" Trent leaned closer to whisper to Rebecca, his hand resting on the butt of his gun.

She nodded, her eyes filled with steely resolve.

Together, they emerged from their hiding place and boarded the boat, weapons drawn. The men on deck flinched at their sudden appearance, raising their hands in surrender and shouting obscenities at Mallard for his betrayal. Among them, Trent recognized Allen Wilson, a name that had cropped up in their investigation time and again. His face was pale, beads of sweat dotting his brow.

"Where are the Sawyers?" Trent's voice thundered across the deck. "They set up this meeting. Tell us now!"

Allen's gaze flickered back and forth between Trent and Rebecca, fear evident in his eyes. "I swear, I don't know. There's been no sign of them yet!"

"Well, if they aren't here, how the hell did the boat get here?"

Before anyone could answer, a dark-haired man ducked low, trying to hide behind the others. He caught Trent's attention.

Realizing he'd been seen, Christoph Blake straightened and adjusted his tie. "We have no idea where they are. We're just waiting for them to arrive before heading farther out to sea. It's standard practice with meetings like these." He gave a hard glare to Mallard before continuing. "We do that to avoid having law enforcement join us. Is there a problem?"

Trent glanced at Rebecca, her brow furrowed in concern. They both knew something was amiss, but what? As the seconds ticked away, Trent checked his watch.

9:59.

It was now or never.

His mind raced, trying to piece together the puzzle before it was too late. He knew the answer was staring him right in the face, barely out of reach. Trent's heart pounded in his chest, the seconds ticking away like a bomb. It was then that the sheriff's station exploding flashed through his mind, the debris and dust filling the air.

Suddenly, it all clicked into place. "Boss, we've got to go! Christian!" He spun around, grabbing Rebecca's arm. "Now!"

"What?" Her gaze swept the area, confusion etched on her face.

"Abandon ship! All of you, get off this boat!" Trent's voice boomed across the deck, urgency fueling him as he dragged Rebecca toward the railing.

"But why? What's going on?" Christian's voice came up from behind them.

"Trust me, Rebecca, jump!" Trent yelled. "Everyone, jump!"

Rebecca plunged into the ocean.

Trent followed suit, slicing through the cold, dark waters beside her. He stayed under the water, swimming as fast as he could. Rebecca was behind him, but she wasn't keeping up. She fell farther behind with every stroke.

As they swam away from the boat as fast as their limbs would allow, a tremendous, earth-shattering explosion rumbled from above the surface. The shockwave hit them like a train, sending them tumbling through the water.

19

The water convulsed, waves rippling outward as the force of the explosion reverberated through its depths. Rebecca and Trent barely made it into the water before the blast came, their bodies somersaulted forward by the shockwave. As she struggled to know which direction led to the surface, Rebecca kicked off her shoes as the waterlogged weight of them pulled her down.

Despite its weight and confining nature, she made the difficult decision to keep her Kevlar vest. It was hell to swim in, but she was certain she'd need every protection to escape this nightmare. Debris rained down around them, each piece a reminder of the narrowly avoided death. At least that determined which way was up.

Dodging it all and fighting against the swirling currents, Rebecca swam to the surface. Her hand struck air, and she kicked hard, driving herself upward.

As her face came loose of the water's hold, she sucked in a deep breath. The air stank of burning gas, sending her mind hurtling back to the events at Little Quell Island. After being ambushed by cartel drug runners, she'd been left alone in the water as she pushed the boat with her men in it toward safety.

The scent acted as a double trigger, recalling the parking garage where she'd been ambushed for the first time. Panic threatened to claw its way up her throat, but she fought it down with sheer determination.

Losing herself in fear wasn't an option, not when lives were at stake. And vomiting while she was trying to swim would be a quick, nasty, and embarrassing way to die.

Rebecca turned to where the brightest light came from. Mallard's boat was engulfed in flames, a sinking pyre that illuminated the chaotic scene. The blast from the large ship had torn through its hull, leaving twisted metal and shattered wood in its wake. People were screaming on board, their cries distorted and muffled. Flames danced across the surface of the water, casting eerie shadows over the survivors.

Something made a splashing sound behind her, and she spun around. Trent was swimming her way.

"Are you okay?" Rebecca had to yell to be heard over the sputtering roar of the flames as more boats caught on fire.

"Think so." His dark eyes reflected the firelight. "You?"

That was the third time Trent had saved her life. Before now, he'd stopped Rod Hammond and then, later, Elaina Roth from sticking her with a knife. This time, he'd somehow deduced there was a bomb on the boat. "I'm okay."

It was hard not to feel grateful, but there simply wasn't time to dwell on it. They needed to get out of the water before the flames reached them or the killer returned.

Christoph Blake's body was floating in a pool of oil, flames melting his hair and lapping at his gaping mouth. She turned away before she had to see his face burn off.

She pushed herself up higher and yelled over the noise of

the inferno, her voice strained with effort. "We need to get out of here. And away from that oil."

"I couldn't agree more. Let's go!" Trent called back. As soon as she'd caught up to him, they swam together toward the closest debris-free area they could find.

She moved through the water, muscles protesting from exhaustion and cramping from the cold. Her arms were constrained by the weight of the waterlogged Kevlar vest. But there was no time to rest. No time to catch her breath.

"Over there!" Rebecca pointed to a floating piece of wood from the wreckage.

They swam toward it. She grabbed hold and was finally able to inhale deeply. Hauling herself out of the water would have to wait until she wasn't so tired, though.

"Keep your eyes peeled." She wiped away the water that clung to her eyelashes. "Anyone we find can swim over here until backup arrives."

"Did you call them in?" Trent reached for his radio, but all he got was static.

Rebecca shook her head. "I'm sure they got the unmistakable message that something went wrong with our plans, though."

Trent nodded, scanning the fiery scene before them.

Rebecca's heart pounded in her ears, distorting the sounds of chaos around her as the relentless ringing threatened to overwhelm her—but then, cutting through the cacophony like a lifeline, she heard the distant hum of an approaching boat.

"Speaking of whom." She breathed deeply, relief flooding her veins. But as the boat drew closer, a cold shiver slithered down her spine. There was only one person on it.

"Rebecca!" Trent hissed, his voice tight with panic. "That's not friendlies!"

Her stomach dropped as her eyes locked onto the man

behind the wheel. Huge, muscular, bald. And he had a gun aimed in the distance.

His gaze was fixed on the burning boats and the screaming survivors like a predator zeroing in on its prey.

"We need to get out of here." She let go of the wood and dove into the dark, murky water.

As soon as Trent joined her, they started swimming away from the burning wreckage. Her lungs screamed for air, but she kept kicking, her muscles straining with effort. Deep water would slow bullets and skew their trajectories while also giving them some cover. Muffled gunfire echoed above, and she prayed the bullets would miss their mark. At least they both had their vests.

After swimming thirty feet or so, she felt the vibrations from the motorboat weakening. It had to be traveling away from them. She grabbed Trent's arm and pulled him closer, signaling that it was safe to go up.

They broke the water's surface, gasping for breath. Without hesitation, Rebecca spun to where she thought the motorboat was. "There!"

Precisely as she feared, the assassin was firing on the survivors. Rebecca pulled her Armory 1911 and returned fire. Her bullets riddled the killer's boat as she was bounced around on the waves. Moments later, Trent's gun joined hers.

The big man ducked for cover, but then he spun the boat around, looking for whoever was shooting at him.

Being so low in the water worked in their favor. He couldn't seem to pinpoint where the shots were coming from. Instead, he fired at random all around them.

"Rebecca, look!" Trent grabbed her attention, and she turned to see Allen Wilson flailing in the water, illuminated by the fiery glow of the sinking ships. The killer hadn't noticed him yet.

"I'll keep the shooter distracted. You go get him to safety."

Rebecca turned as she heard the roar of another engine, this one going much faster. Her deputies were coming to their rescue. Their shots joined the symphony of sounds, and the killer dropped to the deck for a moment.

"There she is!" Viviane screamed as the boat drew close. "We're coming, Rebecca. Hold on!"

Hoyt was at the helm. Greg and Viviane stood near the bow, shooting at the assassin.

Greg ran over to the side of the boat where Jake was. "Get ready!" Jake leaned over the edge, reaching down.

Rebecca stretched up, kicking as hard as she could. Greg and Jake grabbed her hands, pulling her up and over the side.

"Trent's still out there. Behind me." Rebecca struggled to make herself heard as she flipped over the side of the boat, face pressed against the fiberglass siding. "He was going to save another survivor."

"On it." Hoyt turned the boat, and it pitched under Rebecca before she could get herself straightened out. She fell, rolling for a moment before she slammed into a set of legs.

"I see him." Greg stepped over her. "Trent. Get ready to have your ass saved again." He leaned over the gunwale, stretching out, Jake at his side.

"I'm out." Viviane dropped her magazine and reached for the spare at her waist.

"We've got to get to Allen Wilson!" Trent yelled to his fellow deputies. "With the gunfire, I couldn't reach him!"

There were three more gunshots, and Rebecca realized none of them came from their boat.

"Get down!" Hoyt's voice came a moment later, mixing with the steady, rapid-fire shots.

But Greg staggered back a step. He'd been hit.

"No!" Rebecca screamed and lunged forward, but not in time to catch the older deputy as he collapsed in front of her.

Blood poured out of his upper chest, just under the base of his throat where the bulletproof vest didn't cover.

"Abner!" Hoyt yelled, his eyes wide with terror as he abandoned the wheel and began firing at the assassin's boat.

Blood mixed with water as Jake hauled Trent aboard.

"Too much gunfire," Trent sputtered. "I couldn't get close enough."

"Viviane, take the wheel. Jake, return fire. Hoyt, see to Greg." Rebecca straightened, pulling her Ruger 22 from her second holster.

Her heart raced as she took in the scene around her—the bloodied form of Greg Abner, the panicked expressions on her deputies' faces, and the chilling knowledge that the assassin was still standing.

She took aim at the other boat, but he was already turning and speeding off.

Hoyt's hands trembled as he pressed them against Greg's wound, trying to staunch the flow of blood.

The bastard was getting away!

"Boss." Trent gasped for air.

Rebecca searched the waters, trying to figure out a way to navigate the debris to chase after him. But when Trent pointed, her heart lurched at the sight of Allen Wilson still flailing helplessly in the water. "Viviane! Over there!" She watched as the boat veered toward the injured man.

"Help me get him up!" Rebecca yelled to Trent, who got on his knees and nodded grimly as he moved to assist her. Their fingers locked around Wilson's arms, hauling him aboard, water cascading off his beaten body. It seemed the bullets had missed him. Panting, he lay on the deck, gasping for breath.

"Thanks," he managed, his voice barely audible over the engine and the distant crackle of the burning boats.

"Stay down," Rebecca barked at him. Her gaze flicked

back to Greg, fear gnawing at her insides. The other boat was gone. So was any trace of victims yelling and screaming. Everyone else was dead, their bodies floating among the debris. One of the corpses wore Mallard's orange windbreaker. So much for giving him a vest.

"Let's get out of here," she said, her voice tinged with desperation. "Viviane, full speed ahead for shore. As close to the bridge as you can get."

The boat surged forward, slicing through the waves toward the island. The cold ocean spray against her face did nothing to clear her head.

Rebecca knelt beside Greg, adding her hands to Hoyt's, trying desperately to stop the flow of blood. From what she could tell, the bullet entered while he'd been leaning over, meaning it hadn't gone straight out the other side, but down through his lungs and other soft organs. She'd seen gunshot victims before, but the knowledge that he might be beyond saving left her momentarily paralyzed.

This couldn't be happening. Greg had come out of retirement to help her get things under control.

"Dammit, Greg," Hoyt growled through gritted teeth, tears streaming down his cheeks as he applied pressure to his friend's wound. "You can't leave us now."

Greg's hand moved on top of theirs, his bloody fingers clutching Rebecca's with a grip too tight for a man in his condition.

"I…"

"Shhh…" Rebecca whispered. "Save your strength."

Blood spattered from Greg's mouth as he tried again. "I… lived…good…" He coughed, his eyes rolling up to the back of his head. After a few seconds, he focused on her. "Good…life. My…time. Not…your…fault."

As wise as he was, Greg was wrong. This was her fault. All of it.

"Shhh…" She hushed him again. "You're not going anywhere, you hear me?"

His lips twitched up, but only for a moment. "Liar. My… time." He tried saying something more, but the blood inside his throat created a gargling noise she couldn't understand. It sounded very much like, "Love you all."

She went with it.

"We love you too. You need to stay with us because we still have so much to learn from you. You're the wisest of us all. We need you, Greg."

"Yeah," Hoyt said, tears and snot running down his face. "Fight, damn you. Don't do this."

Greg's lips twitched again. "Save…island." The hand on top of hers loosened its grip as he lost consciousness.

Like the good law enforcement officer he was, Sheriff Deputy Greg Abner wasn't thinking about himself in his final moments. He was thinking of others. Of his island.

Rebecca leaned in, her words for his ears alone, a solemn vow in the quiet that followed the storm of urgency. "This is the last stand, Greg," she whispered, her voice steady with resolve. "The last Shadow's siege the Yacht Club will ever force upon us."

It was more than a promise. It was an oath, a commitment that Greg's final plea would not go unanswered.

And she would keep that promise, inspired by the memory of a man who gave everything for the place he called home.

20

Rebecca scanned the shore for any sign of the ambulance Jake had radioed for on their way over. The boat's engine sputtered as Viviane pulled it up to the service dock off Coastal Drive. Since it was mainly used by the DOT, the dock was no-frills and only large enough for one boat. However, it did have a paved, graded path to the road to facilitate moving equipment. It was the perfect place to meet the ambulance.

It was hard judging the distance, and everyone who had a free hand had their flashlights out to help guide her to the unlit landing.

Hoyt stayed knelt over the unconscious Greg, pressing against the wound in his friend's chest and doing his best to keep him alive.

Rebecca and Trent jumped onto the rain-slicked dock, each holding one of the mooring lines tightly. Her socks squelched on the wooden planks, and she looked over to her deputy to make sure she was tying the boat off properly.

"Now twist that loop and feed the tail through it. And pull

it tight." Trent's voice was steady as he guided her through tying the boat off, though his eyes stayed on Hoyt as he kept pressure on Greg's wound.

No sooner had they secured the vessel than an armada of fire trucks and the wailing siren of the ambulance pierced the night air. Jake had provided details to dispatch about the location and nature of the explosion.

"I'll steady the boat. You help the EMTs get down here." Rebecca squatted, using her legs to keep the boat pressed tight against the dock.

Trent took off toward land without another word. The outline of his Kevlar vest was clear through his soaking-wet uniform.

Vests helped, but there were still too many places it didn't cover.

Hearing the clomp of boots on wood, Rebecca turned to see paramedics rushing down the dock with a gurney in tow, their faces tense with urgency.

"Single gunshot wound upper right quadrant," Hoyt barked out, moving with them.

"Sir, can you tell me your name? Can you hear me?" The headlights of the ambulance framed them all in a brilliant glow as one of the EMTs started her routine questions without slowing down.

"Can the rest of you keep this boat steady?" the second EMT asked, lifting a disassembled, bright-yellow scoop stretcher over to the other EMT.

Jake and Viviane climbed out, helping Rebecca stabilize as they moved back and forth, working quickly.

"Okay, we're ready to lift." One of the medics alerted everyone they'd be on the move.

The EMTs and Hoyt were holding the handles of the scoop stretcher. "Keep it steady."

Rebecca pushed harder with her legs, her fingers hooked on the rim of the boat. Viviane and Jake matched her as the first EMT stepped out.

Rebecca glanced up. Greg's eyes were closed, but she was filled with relief as his chest continued to rise and fall, even a little. Once the EMTs and Hoyt were clear, they lifted Greg onto the waiting stretcher.

"Finish buckling him as we go."

"I'm coming with him." Hoyt stared at the woman who'd spoken as if daring her to deny him.

"Fine," the second EMT barked, grabbing straps as she pushed the gurney with her chest. "Keep up and help us keep him stable."

There was no response needed as Hoyt ran alongside the gurney through the light rain and up to the waiting ambulance.

With that taken care of, Rebecca let go of the boat, dropped down, and sat on the dock. There was nothing she could do for Greg at this point, so she shifted her focus to the next problem. They were in over their heads. It was time to call for backup.

Fumbling for her phone, she cursed under her breath when she discovered it was dead. "Someone loan me your phone."

Trent reached for his pocket and pulled out a dripping phone as well.

"Here." Jake handed her his.

Rebecca wiped Greg's blood on her pants before taking it, dialing from memory.

It was late, but Rhonda still answered, her voice heavy with sleep. "This is Lettinger."

"Rhonda, we need help. Boats, rescue, cruisers. Everything you can send us."

"Rebecca?" There was a tinge of surprise in Rhonda's voice. "What happened?"

"Too much to explain in detail over the phone. We've got several dead and floating. There was a bomb on a boat. Several yachts were taken out. We barely made it out alive. And I don't even have a sheriff's station to work out of."

"I heard about the bomb at the station. You're saying there was another bomb?"

"Yes." Rebecca nodded, suddenly aware of how sore she was. The water had absorbed a lot of the concussive force of the bomb, but not all of it. "It was an ambush. Against the Yacht Club. An attempt to take them all out."

She glanced over at Trent. He was standing ramrod straight, staring at the ambulance as it turned around and left the parking lot.

"Well, shit. That's a lot to deal with." Rhonda paused, and Rebecca wondered if she was getting dressed. "I'll get search and rescue boats en route. Send me the location. I've got K-9 troopers heading to the bridge. The first ones will set up a checkpoint looking for explosives. I'll send the rest to you. Where are you?"

"I'm sitting on the dock just to the north of the bridge once you hit the island. Soaking wet, sore, and missing my shoes."

There was a pause. "Yeah, sounds like a really rough night. I'm on my way. Wait for me."

"No choice about that. My cruiser's on the other end of the island." Rebecca hung up, her heart pounding in her chest as she sent Rhonda a text with the longitude and latitude of the meeting site-turned-massacre.

The night's events had spiraled far beyond anything she'd anticipated, and the thought of facing the enemy with their current resources felt like an insurmountable task. But now, at least, backup was on the way.

"Rhonda's sending help." She tried to stand, but her socks got snagged in the weather-worn wood. Cursing under her breath, she stripped the wet cotton from her feet. "They'll go to the wreckage and look for survivors. She's also going to send some officers down to meet us here."

Jake reached down, offering her a hand up. Rebecca took it, grateful for the help. On the boat, Viviane stood alongside Allen Wilson, who shivered, his haunted eyes darting around the scene.

An uneasy silence settled over the group. Rebecca stared at the reflection of the moon rippling on the dark water, her mind racing. The dock creaked beneath them, its age evident in every groan and sway.

"Maybe the Sawyers will bail after this." Viviane's hopeful voice broke the heavy silence. "They've now made enemies out of any survivors of the Yacht Club. What makes you so sure they're going to stick around when all the police show up?"

"Survivors?" Allen Wilson scoffed bitterly, shivering in the night air. "There are no survivors. I'm the only one who listened when Trent said jump."

"I meant the Yacht Club members back on shore," Viviane clarified.

"That's what I'm saying. There aren't any. Everyone was on that yacht."

Shock rippled through the group like a wave crashing on the shore. The only sound for a few moments was the creak of ropes and the slosh of water up the side of the boat.

"Yacht Club members have been disappearing for a while now." Wilson shook his head sorrowfully, his eyes distant. "The marina is full of empty yachts. I think the entire point of that meeting was to cut all their loose ends at once, the few of us who were still left. Well, they missed one."

Rebecca glanced at Viviane, Trent, and Jake, who

exchanged grim looks. She turned back to Wilson. "What do you know about the Sawyer family?"

Wilson hesitated, his eyes sliding away.

Rebecca leaned forward to get his attention. "They tried to murder you, Allen."

He sighed, running a hand through his wet hair. "I only know a little bit. Recently, I've heard rumors that they're the ones who've been running the Yacht Club."

Recently? So they hadn't been running it the whole time. Or Allen Wilson simply didn't know about it until now.

"They tend to stay in the background. I've seen Jim at a couple of boat parties. Vera rarely comes to them. But I know they're often out on long trips." Wilson shifted his gaze to stare at the ocean. "They're the ones in charge of recruiting and training the entertainment."

Rebecca's stomach knotted. "Entertainment? Do you mean the underage girls who are exploited during your little parties?"

"No." His voice was firm as he shook his head in denial. "Though sometimes they recruit from that group. Those are only the party favors. The ones we pimp out to our guests to keep them happy or use for blackmail."

This was going to get worse. Rebecca knew it in her guts.

"The 'entertainment' are the lifers. I'm not going to mince words, but I also can't prove anything. They train young men and women into being good little slaves. So they can be sold for higher profits. The trained ones usually live longer in their new homes, too, from what I've heard."

That made sense out of a lot of things Rebecca had learned. But to hear it was her ex-boyfriend's parents who were in charge of it was sickening.

"Was that their yacht that exploded out there?" Rebecca did her best to sound authoritative, though she didn't feel especially assertive, standing there barefoot.

"I'm not sure, but I think so. I didn't even think to look at the name of the boat. It was where we were told to meet up, so I climbed aboard. Things like that aren't exactly unusual." He plucked at his sodden clothes.

"Dammit." She thought of their pen cameras, then realized hers and Trent's were probably dead after their ocean swim. "We'll have to use Greg, Viviane, Jake, and Hoyt's cameras and see if any of them captured the name of the boat that went up in flames."

"One thing I do know, Jim and Vera have more than one yacht," Wilson said.

"Would you be willing to testify against them?" Rebecca's gaze forced the man to turn and look at her.

Wilson hesitated again before responding in a shaken voice. "They always get what they want."

Rebecca laughed, a bitter edge to the sound. "I've heard that a lot, but I haven't seen much proof of it."

"Proof?" His eyebrows shot up. "What do you mean?"

"Vera and Jim wanted Vale to win the election, the party girls to keep showing up, me dead, and all of you gone tonight." She ticked off points on her fingers. "And yet, here we are, still breathing. It would appear they don't always get what they want. If they're going to get what they want in the end, you're going to die regardless. So you might as well cooperate."

Wilson swallowed hard, his gaze flicking from Rebecca to the others. "If you can keep me safe, I'll testify. I have some documents that could be used as evidence. But I need your promise that you'll protect me."

"Promise?" Rebecca echoed, her voice soft yet resolute. "You have my word, Allen. We'll keep you safe."

Can I, though?

She hadn't kept Greg safe, and he'd only been serving as backup for the primary mission. And who knew how many more had been blown to bits by the boat explosion? She might not be able to keep Allen Wilson safe, but she'd do what she could.

Flashing lights on the bridge announced several troopers coming their way.

"Looks like our ride is nearly here. We'll all go to the hospital, get checked out, and figure out what to do next."

21

Rebecca's muscles ached as she stepped into the waiting room, still wearing the wet, tattered clothes from earlier. Some mild muscle relaxers had started to work their magic, but she knew it would be some time before she felt anywhere near normal again. She needed updates on Greg, and she made her way out to the waiting room.

Hoyt paced back and forth, his brow furrowed in concern. On seeing Rebecca, he stopped. "I haven't heard anything yet." He cut her off before she had a chance to ask her question. "And I called Elijah, Greg's son and his only family now. He's on his way from Chesapeake. Works as a deep-sea underwater welder, but he's not working right now, so I was able to get ahold of him directly. He's shaken up but swears he's okay to drive."

"It's tough to get that kind of news." Rebecca knew that from firsthand experience. She felt sorry for Elijah. But he wasn't the only one who was close to Greg. After losing Wallace, Hoyt and Greg had grown even closer. "How are you holding up?"

"Okay, I guess." Hoyt ran a hand through his hair.

"Abner's a good man, a good deputy. I've known him for decades. On the ambulance ride over, I thought we'd lost him for sure. But I'm hoping for the best." He looked down at the floor. "Maybe this is the wrong time to bring it up, but I've been thinking about retiring. Angie agrees with me. Poor Greg was retired, and look at him now."

Rebecca couldn't blame him, though her heart cracked at the thought of working without Hoyt by her side.

"Things will calm down soon," she reassured him. "Once we deal with the Yacht Club, things will get better. They have to." Looking around, she realized they were the only two people there waiting. "Where's Locke? Is he still being checked out?"

"Viviane and Jake are working with the state police on the island." Hoyt not-so-subtly avoided the question about Trent.

Before Rebecca could press further, Angie burst into the waiting room, a dark-blue nylon bag clutched in her hands. She rushed to Hoyt, planting a quick kiss on his cheek.

"Any word yet?"

"Nothing yet. But it's bad, Ange." Hoyt reached for her hand, and she squeezed him tightly.

"We can always pray for a miracle. Let's not give up hope." She turned to Rebecca and held up the bag. "Here. Viviane told me where to find your spare uniform in your cruiser and asked me to bring it over. She told me everything that happened tonight."

"Thank you, Angie." Rebecca was touched by the gesture. She recalled how Angie and Lilian Hudson had cobbled together her first utility belt. The memory brought a bittersweet smile to her face.

Angie then handed her a bag of couscous, which left Rebecca momentarily puzzled.

"Drop your phone in it," Angie instructed, shaking the bag. "It's better than rice. It'll dry out any remaining water."

Rebecca nodded, grateful. "Great idea. Thanks."

Angie twisted another bag in her hands. "I brought one for Trent, too, but I haven't seen him. Where is he, dear?"

Hoyt snorted and seemed to be chewing on his tongue. "Trent's always late or leaving early, especially when it comes to hospitals."

Rebecca knew he was talking about the night Wallace had been shot. Trent had ridden in the ambulance to the hospital and said he'd stay there to make sure everyone was updated. Instead, he'd left early without warning. She and Hoyt had sat in the waiting room that night, getting to know each other as they waited for news.

Though she understood where he was coming from, she owed it to Trent to correct Hoyt. "Except tonight was nothing like the last time. Trent saved my life. He figured out there was a bomb on the boat and got me out of there. And he lost a friend in the process."

"I didn't think about that." Hoyt's expression softened, guilt creeping into his eyes. "I'm still wary, but I'll try to go easy on him. This whole thing with Ryker and his family has me distrusting everyone." He hesitated before adding, "I will say, Trent's shaping up. A lot of that is Greg's doing. Not much of a legacy, but it's something, at least."

Angie rubbed Hoyt's back soothingly as they all stood around, the silence punctuated by the steady buzz of nurses and staff as they went about their normal routines.

That was always the worst part of being in a hospital. Worried friends and family felt so emotional as they waited, but for everyone else, they had to be professional and continue to go about their business.

A doctor emerged from the ER, spotted Rebecca's uniform, and approached her. "Are you Sheriff West?"

Rebecca's heart pounded in her ears as the doctor, a middle-aged woman with tired eyes and a somber expression, delivered the news they'd all been dreading. "Yes."

"I'm sorry." Her voice was barely more than a whisper. "Deputy Greg Abner didn't make it. The damage to his heart was too severe."

The weight of those words crashed down on them like an unrelenting wave, silencing everything with an overwhelming white noise. Angie squeezed Hoyt's hand, and he wrapped an arm around her waist. The couple held each other up as they tried to absorb what they'd just learned.

This couldn't be happening again.

First Alden Wallace, then Darian Hudson, now Greg Abner. Greg, who had only come back to active duty because she'd asked him to. He'd been retired. He should be sitting on his boat, drinking beers and fishing. Not lying dead in a hospital.

Before anyone could respond, Trent limped into the waiting room, his body stiff from the earlier ordeal, his clothes soaked with ocean water. His dark eyes were filled with a desperate hope, searching for any sign of good news.

But when he saw their stricken faces and the doctor's solemn demeanor, that hope crumbled, replaced by a raw, silent grief. Tears welled up in his eyes, and he choked out a plea to Rebecca. "No. Tell me it's not true. Tell me Greg's alive, that he's going to be fine."

Rebecca's mouth opened, but no words came out. She couldn't bring herself to confirm what Trent already knew. Sensing the tension, the doctor took her leave, slipping away to attend to other patients.

"Boss. West, please," Trent begged again, his voice breaking. "Tell me Greg didn't die trying to save my worthless life."

Hoyt, unable to contain his own emotions, let out a heartbroken sob. He'd known Greg for decades. With a bond that transcended friendship, they'd become something akin to brothers—and now, just like that, Greg was gone.

Trent looked at Hoyt, anguish etched across his face, and walked over to him. Rebecca wasn't sure what was going to happen.

Trent opened and closed his mouth a few times before he managed to croak out, "Dammit, Hoyt. I am so damned sorry. It should've been me."

"No." Hoyt clenched his jaw as tears streamed down. "He wanted to save you. And he did. That's what he wanted. Don't you ever feel bad about that."

Hoyt reached out with his free arm and pulled Trent in. They embraced, two men bound together by shared loss and pain, supporting each other as their tears flowed freely.

Angie and Rebecca stood nearby, feeling the heavy burden of grief settle on their shoulders as well. Angie rubbed Hoyt's back as she watched her husband and Trent cry. It was a scene that would forever be seared in Rebecca's mind.

Rebecca's emotions were a whirlwind. Anger at the Yacht Club, the party responsible for this tragedy. Stark fear for the safety of her friends and colleagues. Sorrow for Greg's son. Things had to change. The violence had to end. They had to stop the Yacht Club once and for all.

But for now, all they could do was grieve for their fallen friend and find strength in one another as they faced an uncertain future.

22

I stood at the bow of the *Blue Liberty*, gripping the railing with anticipation. I didn't even mind the light rain that had begun to fall. It meant more fog, and that was to my benefit. The night was cold and unforgiving, the sea breeze chilling me to the bone. In years past, the breeze off the ocean had exhilarated me, but now, it was too cold to handle.

Through my binoculars, I'd watched as the *Delilah* exploded in a fiery spectacle. The heat of the flames had dispersed the fog…until the smoke clouded my view. Then the sound of gunfire echoed across the water, mixed with the distant cries of men. Through it all, my worthless son had stood beside me, horrified, looking seasick.

After the show was over, Jim had changed course, taking us south again to where we could remain mostly out of sight from the island. And so, we waited.

Then, in the distance, I heard another boat approaching, and it made my heart race.

Hopefully, Archer had killed everyone just as Jim and I had planned. But more than confirmation of the kills, I longed for the details.

A perverse thrill coursed through my veins as I imagined the carnage unfolding on the doomed vessel. The thought of all those lives snuffed out simultaneously left me hot and bothered, despite the biting wind. It truly was a pity we'd had to dispatch the members of the club all at once. I was robbed of the opportunity to experience this thrill for each kill separately.

Returning from his mission, Archer approached from the lower decks. His smile brightened as his eyes landed on me.

"And…how did it go?"

He looked uncharacteristically sheepish, his muscular frame tense. This was not an appealing side of him. "I blew up the boat. Everyone aboard died. The ones who were thrown overboard drowned while burning. If they seemed to be taking too long, I put a bullet in them to speed it along."

"Good job."

His tongue flicked out to wet his lips, sending a thrill between my legs. "I'd show you their dismembered pieces, but they're likely on the sea floor by now. Being eaten by the fish and crabs."

"What about that bitch of a sheriff?" I glanced at my worthless son, who'd failed me repeatedly. He seemed as interested in Archer's answer as I was.

Ryker had destroyed my fantasy about him strangling Rebecca while they slept together. But dying in a fiery explosion when she thought she was about to win would be almost as good.

Archer hesitated. "She showed up with a deputy, just like we were hoping. But something must've spooked them, because they jumped overboard right before I detonated the blast."

I clenched my jaw. "And then you gunned them down in the water, right?"

Grimacing, Archer shook his head. "No. I couldn't find

them at first. And by the time I did, the other deputies had showed up and started shooting at me. I had to get out of there before they sank my boat."

Anger roiled my insides as yet another person disappointed me. I needed to know more. "How many of the members were on board? How many boats?"

"From what I could see, there were ten men on board. Only a handful of boats, so they must've ridden out together." Archer looked steadier now that I'd pivoted the conversation away from his failure to eliminate the sheriff.

I'd very clearly conveyed how much I wanted that woman dead and how many times she'd managed to slip out of my traps.

Still, Rebecca hadn't been the main target tonight. Archer had been watching from a distance. Although he'd gotten closer than I dared hope, his body count was likely inaccurate due to his distance. I turned to my loyal husband, who was silently watching. "It's time you get us the hell away from this island. Our moles say they have recorded confessions." I glared at my useless son. "Thanks to you, you ungrateful snitch."

Ryker retched over the side, and his weakness annoyed me. Clearly, the sniveling weakling feared my retribution. And he should.

Archer opened his mouth as if to say something, hesitated, then closed it again.

My cold-blooded killer was acting off. Pulling me from my fantasies about punishing Ryker. This wasn't the man who inspired so much longing in me earlier. "What is it?"

"One of the guys jumped overboard," Archer admitted. "I shot at him. But since he was in the water, I couldn't confirm the kill. He went down, but that isn't as conclusive as I'd like it to be. And I couldn't wait around to see if he came back up. I was under heavy fire."

"Give me his description." I was paying top dollar for Archer to be flawless. No one seemed able to measure up except my dear Jim.

As Archer described the man, my heart sank. Allen Wilson knew I was in charge of the club. This new development threatened my power and my life.

I gripped the railing of the yacht, trying to contain my rage. "I thought you were a professional. You're being paid handsomely for a reason."

Archer's cheeks flushed red, and he struggled to meet my gaze.

My useless son made a noise. I turned to see him leaning against the cabin wall with a small smile on his lips.

I rounded on him. "Are you enjoying this? Is everyone in this godforsaken club completely incompetent? Do I need to do everything around here?" I wasn't playing around. Maybe I'd get even more pleasure from killing these people myself.

"Mother." Ryker's voice was pathetically low. "I don't think you're as smart as—"

"Enough!" I spun toward Archer, who seemed to have regained some composure. "You'd better take care of this mess. You're supposed to be a pro. Finish the job you started."

"I will." His voice was steady again. "I'm a professional, and I'll make sure Allen Wilson's taken care of. I won't leave anyone alive who could harm you."

Though it was risky to continue to trust others, Archer was certainly dedicated to making things right with me. "See that you do. Because if you don't, you'll end up on the sea floor, too, the same as those sorry bastards you blew up. I might not kill my own son, but you're a different story."

Archer nodded, his expression somber. "I understand." He seemed filled with shame at having failed me. His attitude adjustment stirred the warmth within me again.

As soon as Archer was out of earshot, getting off the yacht and onto his boat, Ryker spoke. "You've gone too far, Mother. Was it really a good idea to threaten to murder a professional assassin?"

"Shut up. You wouldn't know anything about this kind of work. You're too soft for it."

Had I pushed Archer too far? He was a skilled killer. Maybe I should've been more cautious.

I shook away the uncertainty. There was no time for second-guessing. The situation was dire, and my empire was being threatened.

"Mother." Ryker's kind, soft voice broke my train of thought. His gaze darted around the boat before settling on me. "I know you're angry, but you've misunderstood. My 'confession' was all lies. To throw them off. We're going to be okay. You're safe. Dad's safe. We'll all be safe soon."

Ah, there's my obedient boy. Maybe he's not as worthless as I thought.

I sighed to release some of the tension that had been building up in my shoulders. "You're right. But we have to act quickly and decisively. Allen Wilson is a loose end that cannot be allowed to unravel."

23

Rebecca's cell phone jolted her awake the next morning, its shrill ring slicing through the fog of sleep like a knife. Pulling the device out of the baggie of dried couscous, she finally answered the call.

"This is West."

"Rebecca, it's Rhonda." Rebecca blinked, struggling to see what time it was. It felt like she'd just fallen asleep. "Can you meet me at the intersection near the bridge as soon as possible? We've got officers stationed outside Allen Wilson's house, and he's still alive and kicking. But I need to go over next steps with you."

"Understood." Rebecca tried not to yawn but failed. "I'll be there as soon as I can." She hung up, struggling to get out of bed with muscles that had stiffened in the night. Humphrey stirred next to her on the comforter. She threw on her spare uniform from the night before and stumbled out to the kitchen, her faithful friend following close behind.

"I can't walk you this morning, but I'll make it up to you." She opened the sliding door to the deck and let the chocolate lab out to relieve himself. He hesitated only a moment before darting out into the rain.

While she waited for coffee to brew, she called Viviane.

A sleepy voice answered. "Hey, Rebecca. Please tell me this is a personal call. I was up 'til two in the morning."

"Sorry, Darby." She used Viviane's last name to make it clear this was work related. "Rhonda called and asked me to meet her near the bridge. I want you to come with me. Trent's still limping, Hoyt's with Elijah Abner, and Jake's still out on the boat."

"I'm starting to think Coffey sleeps as little as you do."

Rebecca ignored Viviane's comment, not bothering to tell her deputy that she'd been out in the field until four and had only gotten five hours of sleep. "Got to love that overtime pay, though, right?"

Viviane snorted. "I do. Jake probably does. But aren't you salaried?"

Rebecca swapped out her coffee pot with her cup as it finally started to drip out of the brew basket. "Salary, yep. But at least they pay for my dry cleaning."

"Really?"

She grinned. "No. So quit complaining and meet me in fifteen minutes."

"Fine. I'm on my way now."

As Rebecca hung up, she moved to the back door and called to Humphrey, who promptly bounded onto the deck, tail wagging. She scratched behind his ears and kissed the top of his head before attempting to dry his damp and sandy feet. "You're such a good boy. Sorry I have to run out." She dumped some leftovers into his bowl before snatching a granola bar from the pantry for herself.

She zombie-walked over to put her shoes on. Everything was a yawn-filled haze as she finished getting ready, climbed into her SUV, and made it over to the rendezvous point.

Rhonda was waiting with a small group of troopers. Rebecca pulled in, parked, and waited as Viviane parked next to her. Together, they walked over to Rhonda. Thankfully, the rain had subsided. But the low-hanging clouds signaled the weather front was sticking around a bit longer.

"My team hasn't found any other survivors." Rhonda studied Rebecca's face. "I know you were on the scene at the time of the explosion. I also know there's been more going on here than what we're cleaning up now. So give me the full story."

Rebecca glanced at Viviane, suddenly glad she'd been the one available to come out today. She wouldn't want to talk about this in front of anyone else. "I haven't told you yet." Rebecca shifted closer, and Viviane's chin jerked up in shock before she shuffled near too. "You remember that guy I was dating?"

Rhonda frowned. "The guy with the nice ass?" Her jaw dropped then snapped shut. "Oh, Rebecca, don't tell me he's involved."

Rebecca flinched. "He's the son of the leaders of the Yacht Club. And I arrested him after he conspired to have me killed in my own bed. Viviane saved me."

"She didn't need my help. Not really. She already had the guy handled." Viviane waved away Rebecca's words.

"Go ahead and tell her." Rebecca sighed. "I really don't want to have to admit it all."

Viviane shot her a compassionate glance and gave Rhonda a succinct breakdown of everything that happened in the last few days. Her own mother, in a coma after her vehicle was sabotaged. Luka Reynold's attempt to kill Rebecca in her own home and Ryker's betrayal. The bomb at the station, the stolen evidence, one prisoner murdered and the other on the lam. The mass murder on the exploding yacht. Greg Abner's death in the line of duty.

"Holy shit." Rhonda put her hand over her mouth as she stared at Ryker's photo on his booking sheet on her tablet. Jim and Vera Sawyer's photos were part of the file as well. "That's a lot. That's a whole lot."

"Yeah, and now it looks like we're having to deal with the death throes of a multimillion-dollar criminal organization that's been operating for the last few decades." Rebecca took a sip of coffee, not only because she needed it, but to cover the emotions playing out on her face.

"I can tell you there's no sign of your psycho ex or his murderous family or their boat yet. Are you sure you're okay? You look like you had a hell of a night after one hell of a week." Rhonda gave her a sympathetic grin.

"I'm fine." Rebecca did her best to assure her, even though the lingering fear and exhaustion had to be hinting otherwise. "Rhonda, can you escort Allen Wilson off the island? Until we catch the Sawyers, keep him in police custody on the mainland, and not in the general population either. It wouldn't be safe. He might be our only witness who can testify against the Sawyers, so we need to keep him alive."

As she spoke, Rebecca realized this was the first time she'd considered that Ryker might be dead or unwilling to testify. The thought sent a cold shiver down her spine. Maybe he deserved death, but she didn't want it to be true.

"Yeah, I've already suggested that to Wilson. He said he's not interested in leaving the island." Rhonda held her hands up before Rebecca could say anything else. "I don't know what his deal is."

"Dammit." Wilson had said he'd cooperate, especially after everything that had happened. "We should go talk to him."

The crisp autumn air carried the threat of continued rain as Rebecca's mind raced with possibilities. If the Sawyers realized Allen Wilson had survived, she knew they wouldn't leave without eliminating whatever threat he posed.

"While Darby and I do that, could you search for Jim, Vera, and Ryker? If they're still here somewhere, we need to find them before they do any more damage. Issue a BOLO for all three across the region, land and sea."

"I can do that. We're still pulling up wreckage, so we have boats all over the place. Visibility is crap, though. The fog rolled in and is, quite frankly, screwing up everything." Rhonda nodded, pulling out her radio to relay the message.

"Check all docks and marinas. They might've switched to another boat. After everything they've done, I wouldn't be surprised if they stole one." She thought about when they'd found the bank robber hiding out in Longfellow's house. "Or they might be using one that belonged to one of their victims."

Rebecca's attention flicked between the officers gathered nearby. She wondered if they knew precisely how vicious the people they were looking for really were.

"We'll need to track down any vehicles they own. That includes any owned by their shell companies. I'm sure they've got a few. And don't rule out the possibility they could be hiding on land. Look into local hotels and guesthouses. Hell, they might even be laying low at their own home."

"Yeah, I got you. No worries." Rhonda waved her people over. "We'll check everything. You go figure out what that Wilson guy is on about. You said he talked to you last night, so get him to talk today."

Rebecca agreed, turning to meet Viviane's gaze. "We need to find out why he doesn't want to cooperate anymore. Hopefully, it's not because someone has gotten in his head already. He's our key to bringing the Sawyers down."

As they started toward Rebecca's SUV, she felt uneasy. Something wasn't adding up. Why would Wilson suddenly refuse to leave the island? He should've been desperate to stay alive, especially given the danger he was in.

24

Sunlight glinted off the water, casting a shimmering reflection on the clapboard siding of Allen Wilson's house. Seeing the sun offered a glimmer of hope to Rebecca's tired body. She and Viviane pulled up in front of the modest, two-story home nestled among the labyrinthine waterways toward the south end of Shadow Island.

"Looks like we're not the only ones here." Viviane indicated the three state police cars parked outside. Troopers sat inside each vehicle, eyes alert and watchful.

Rebecca rolled down her window and addressed the closest trooper. "Has Wilson left his house at all today?"

"No, ma'am." The trooper's gaze never left the house. The wide and irregular yard gave a view to the back where a small motorboat gently bobbed by a private dock.

"We're going to go have a word with him and see if we can talk him into moving somewhere more secure. Keep an eye out. Thanks." Rebecca rolled up the window and stepped out of the cruiser.

She approached the door and rapped sharply.

Almost immediately, Wilson's panicked voice rang out. "I'm not answering!"

"Allen Wilson, it's Sheriff Rebecca West. We spoke last night when we pulled you out of the water." She spoke loudly and directly into the door so he could hear her, doing her best to sound reassuring. "We need to talk."

The door cracked open barely enough for Wilson's suspicious eyes to peer out. On seeing Rebecca, his expression brightened, and he swung the door open wider. "Have you caught those damn Sawyers yet?" His tone was a mix of hope and fear as he beckoned them inside.

"Unfortunately, no." Rebecca and Viviane stepped into the house.

Another one of Rhonda's state police officers stood near the window in the den, peering through the blinds at their surroundings with an air of unease.

Rebecca got straight to the point. "But I thought we had a deal, Wilson. I saved your life, you testify against the organization, and you walk free once the Sawyers are arrested."

"We still have that deal, I promise." Wilson wrung his hands nervously. His eyes darted to the window, as if expecting a sniper's bullet at any moment. It was a realistic fear, considering what had happened to Jay Griles.

"Then why won't you go with Special Agent Lettinger to the mainland?" Viviane's voice was tinged with exasperation. "You'd be safer there."

"Sure, if I ever get there," Wilson replied cryptically.

Rebecca and Viviane exchanged puzzled glances before turning their attention back to him for an explanation.

"Jay Griles thought he'd be safe on the mainland too. That's where he told me he was going." Allen's voice trembled. "And look where that got him."

"Griles tried to run on his own with no protection. He didn't have an armed police escort guiding him." Rebecca pointed to the trooper who was pretending he wasn't listening to their every word. She tried to keep the mounting frustration out of her voice. "You've got at least four here now. We can get more if you want, and they'll drive you to safety."

Wilson's fear seemed undiminished. In the silence that followed, Rebecca could almost hear the gears turning in his head, calculating the risks and probabilities of survival.

"The Sawyers have more resources than we thought. I mean, they blew up a bunch of boats with one bomb! They blew up your station! Who's to say they don't have more?" Wilson's gaze darted around the room as he spoke, his voice barely more than a whisper as he leaned in close. "What if the staties are on their payroll? What if they blow up the car with me inside? Or the bridge as I'm going over it?"

Rebecca watched him closely, noting the beads of sweat forming on his forehead and the way his hands trembled. He wasn't exaggerating or trying to pull one over on them. The man was genuinely terrified.

"Allen, if the troopers were on Vera's payroll, they'd have already killed you." She glanced at Viviane, who looked ready to strangle Allen Wilson out of sheer annoyance. Her fingers kept twitching like they were searching for a throat. Rebecca knew that wouldn't help matters, but she couldn't deny the temptation was there. Instead, she took a deep breath and tried to reason with him one last time.

"Staying here is not any safer. The Sawyers know where you live. They could blow up your house right now. Griles was killed near his house." But as she spoke, she knew in her heart that this was a battle she wasn't going to win.

"Then I'd rather die in my home than in a cop car." He looked around his house, and Rebecca had to admit, it was a well-decorated and comfortable looking place. "I'm less exposed here. And if the cops really are here to protect me, it'll be easier to protect my house than a car."

Rebecca clenched her jaw, realizing she wasn't going to get through to him. She wished she had a reason to arrest him and force him to leave, but that would only risk jeopardizing his future testimony. "What do you want us to do, then?"

A glimmer of hope flickered in Wilson's eyes. "Catch Vera and Jim first, or the man who shot at us last night. Then I'll feel much safer. You've done it before. I'm sure you can do it again." He laughed, a tinge of panic in his voice. "In fact, I'm betting my life on your ability to do so, Sheriff."

Rebecca sighed, knowing she didn't have many options. "If I catch them, then you'd be willing to testify?" While they didn't have solid evidence against them for a specific crime, Rebecca could always bring them in on suspicion…though maybe she could do better than that. "Will you at least start to give your testimony now? That'll help us press charges against them."

"How would I do that?" Wilson blinked owlishly at her, and Rebecca wondered if the man had slept at all.

"This is your house. I'm sure you have pen and paper here. Start writing down what you know. Any crimes you know that either Jim or Vera were involved in." She knew the task would also give him something to focus on, so he wouldn't be working himself into a frenzy.

"I can do that." He nodded rapidly. "I'll write down everything I know. And you catch Vera and Jim. And that way, the case will move forward fast, and I can get out of this mess once and for all." Wilson rubbed his fingers against his thumbs and turned his head to the side. "Um, like, should I write out that Jim told me to vandalize all those houses?"

"What do you mean?" It took Rebecca a moment to remember the cases of vandalism that had plagued the island a few weeks ago. They'd thought it was teens acting out at the time. "You were the one doing all that? Why?"

Wilson flinched. "They wanted to target your supporters to prove you couldn't protect them. I even signed it with the name of my boat, so people knew it was someone from the Yacht Club doing it." His voice trailed off at the end.

Signature? She tried to remember if she'd seen anything like that. Then she remembered the crude drawings. They hadn't understood what they'd represented, but knowing Wilson was behind it made everything fall into place. He was trying to draw a humanized clam that was working as a stripper to represent Wilson's yacht, the *Clam Strips*.

Rebecca snorted at the irony. "And now you're relying on me and my men to keep you safe. I bet you really regret that now."

"More than you could ever understand." He nodded. "And it didn't work anyway."

"Yes, put that down too. And anything else they ordered you to do." Rebecca turned to leave, Viviane following behind her.

She stepped through the door to go hold up her end of the bargain, Viviane on her heels. As it slammed shut behind them, she heard both locks get thrown.

Once outside, Viviane couldn't contain her frustration any longer. "Can you believe how stupid he's being?"

"Darby, think about it." She considered the three cop cars parked outside and thought of the officers who had lost their lives. Truthfully, she could understand why Allen Wilson was acting the way he was.

Rebecca explained her logic. "Three months ago, there were so many Yacht Club members, we filled whole filing cabinets about them. Last month, there were still plenty of them left, and even two days ago, the big players were all alive. And now Wilson's the only one left. I'd be scared shitless, too, if all my friends had died."

Rebecca herself had "only" lost three people, Sheriff Wallace, Darian Hudson, and Greg Abner. And that was enough to spook her. She was already sleeping with a gun under her pillow every night, and she couldn't relax until Humphrey settled down beside her. Her own fear tried to gnaw at her insides, but she pushed it down, determined to keep going.

As Viviane made her way to the cruiser and climbed in, she frowned hard enough to wrinkle her forehead and pull her eyebrows down. Rebecca got in, started the engine, and pulled onto the road. "I guess I never really thought of the Yacht Club assholes as people. Not really. Not ones who had friends or people who would care after they died."

"Criminals get to have friends, family, and loved ones too. And losing so many of them so quickly is going to shake anyone up. The Yacht Club was Wilson's entire way of life, and that's gone. He's lost his coworkers and friends. And he knows his neck is the next one on the chopping block."

"But we don't know that." Viviane's voice was soft. "He's not the only person the Yacht Club tried and failed to kill. You were too. And so was Trent."

"All the more reason to catch them as fast as we can." Rebecca drove down the road. The light breaking through the clouds sent patterns dancing on the waterways near Wilson's house, and yet the beauty of the view couldn't dispel the darkness that had enveloped Shadow Island.

25

Rebecca maneuvered her cruiser through the winding roads of Shadow Island, heading for the lot where she'd met Rhonda earlier. She reached for her radio, needing an update from the cleanup crew.

Although unlikely, there was still a slim chance Greg's or Viviane's return fire had taken out the shooter. Since the throttle on his boat would've stayed engaged, he would've seemed alive as his boat motored away.

Jake responded to her hail. "We haven't fished up any bodies I can't identify, Boss."

"Locke, are you out there too?" She was slightly distracted by the autumn foliage around her.

"Affirmative, Sheriff." Trent's usually quiet voice came through a touch strained. "Coffey and I are working with Lettinger's people, investigating the wreckage. We're still collecting bodies and potential pieces of evidence."

Rebecca's eyebrows shot up in surprise. She'd expected Trent to be home, recovering from the explosion that had rattled them all. "Didn't think you'd be back at it so soon, Locke. What have you found?"

"Other than the expected bodies, we've confirmed the identity of the boat. This one is the *Delilah*. The experts are confirming that the scorch marks on it indicate it's where the bomb was planted. I'll keep you updated if we find anything else."

"Thanks, Locke. Stay safe out there." As she hung up the radio, she felt that same itch again, the feeling that they were missing something crucial. "Darby, can you look up that name? Find out who owns it."

Viviane spun the computer around and started her search. A few clicks later, she found what she was looking for. "The *Delilah* is one of the boats Rhonda flagged as being owned by a shell company, like you thought. But her people were able to track it back to Jim Sawyer." Which was also what they'd expected. "But there's another yacht listed under the same LLC. This one is twice the size and named *Blue Liberty*."

That was probably where Ryker and his parents were hiding. The question was, where? They could be anywhere by now. There was no reason to assume they were hanging around. And so far, they'd only tracked down those two boat names. As Hoyt kept telling her, she needed to understand what it meant to live on an island.

Boats weren't merely a means of employment or transportation. They could also be homes.

Or headquarters.

Could Jim and Vera be calling the shots from this second yacht? Their house was under surveillance. No one had seen any sign of them there.

Thankfully, she knew a man who could tell her all about yachts and their owners. Changing her course, she headed for Seaview Marina.

She turned to Viviane. "We need to speak with Lewis Longmire. There's a yacht we need to inquire about."

They were already close, and within a couple of minutes, they were pulling into the parking lot of the Seaview Marina, home and headquarters to the Yacht Club.

"Keep your eyes open. The killer could be hiding out here, looking for stragglers. Longmire might also be a target. Despite him not being a member, he still knows a lot of the comings and goings of the members."

Viviane took a quick breath. "Yeah, Boss. Enemy territory here. I'm not about to forget these are the people who tried to kill my mother, no matter who else might be their friends."

It was a bitter and biased thing for her to say, but Rebecca couldn't blame her. Seeing Meg, Viviane's sweet-as-honey mother, hooked up to machines to monitor her recovery made her want retribution as well.

Greg's face swam into her mind, and she closed that shit down. She couldn't think of the dear older deputy right then. She'd catch the bastards who'd killed him before mourning her friend.

And avenge them all.

Luka Reynold had been the man who sabotaged Meg's car, but he'd done it under orders from the Yacht Club. Or more directly, Vera or Jim Sawyer. She climbed out of the vehicle and made her way to the door of the marina's main building. The salty air whipped their hair around their faces as they kept scanning the area for threats. The scent of seaweed and diesel fuel filled their nostrils.

"Remember, he might not be as cooperative as we'd like." Rebecca adjusted her gun holster before entering the building. "But we need to find out if that yacht's still docked here. If he won't tell us, we'll have to find a reason to walk down the pier and look for it."

"We can always tell him we're here to collect the property from the people who died last night."

Together, they walked into Seaview Marina, ready to confront whatever lay ahead in their pursuit of justice.

The building was not only empty of people, it was completely silent. Even the Muzak that had played through the hidden speakers last time Rebecca visited was absent. "If there's even anyone to ask. Longmire's office is down this hall. Let's check there."

She pushed open the door to his office. Perched behind a cluttered desk, Lewis Longmire looked like a ghost of his former self. Though haggard and scared, he still wore an impeccably pressed suit, as if clinging to the last vestiges of his dignity.

"Longmire." Rebecca's greeting was tense but controlled. "We need information."

He looked up, dark circles underlining his tired eyes. "What do you want?"

Rebecca walked up to the first chair across from him, the one she'd sat in last time, and dropped into it.

Viviane set herself up in the doorway like a bodyguard.

"Last night, there was an accident offshore. I'm looking into the cause. What can you tell me about Jim and Vera Sawyer?"

Longmire shrugged, his shoulders sagging beneath his suit. "Not much. They've got a couple of boats docked here."

Rebecca frowned, disbelief flickering across her face. She'd expected resistance, not this easy compliance. Glancing at Viviane, who shared her surprise, she pressed on. "Just the two boats? The *Delilah* and the *Blue Liberty*?"

"Uh, yeah." Longmire rubbed his temples. "I can show you where they're usually docked."

"Wait." Rebecca utterly failed to conceal her shock. "You're going to help us, just like that?"

Longmire let out a hollow laugh, the sound rattling around the cramped office like the wind outside. "Your words have haunted me, Sheriff. As more and more of my clients died, I realized the truth. Do you remember what you told me back then?"

Rebecca opened and closed her mouth, trying to remember exactly what she'd said months ago. She'd been angry at the time, and her memory of it was a bit vague. So much had happened since.

"Let me remind you. 'If you're not a part of the gang, then you're not protected by them either.'"

A chill crawled down Rebecca's spine. "I remember."

"I should've listened to you then. You tried to warn me, but I was too blind to see. The Yacht Club's a group of thugs, and they don't value human life. Ask me anything. I'll tell you what I know."

Rebecca leaned forward to rest her forearms on her knees. "And you once told me, 'When kings and queens fight, their servants die first.'"

He looked at her with troubled eyes. "I did say that. But I'm no longer their servant. I have no clients. All memberships have been terminated as of today."

Longmire's gaze fell to the piles of paper on his desk. "Because they're all dead. This marina has become a graveyard of the Atlantic, and I can't be its caretaker any longer. Let me show you the boats still moored here with living owners. That should tell you everything you need to know."

He stood up and walked out of the office.

Viviane widened her eyes, staring out the door he'd just walked through. She mouthed, *What the hell?*

Rebecca shrugged and strode out as well.

As she and Viviane followed Longmire through the dimly lit hallway, Rebecca felt the weight of their investigation settle on her shoulders. She shared a glance with Viviane, whose eyes mirrored her own resolve.

Rain beat down on the marina, casting a shimmering reflection on the water as Rebecca, Viviane, and Longmire headed out to the docks. He'd stopped to grab an umbrella and gestured for them to take one from the umbrella stand as well. Viviane grabbed one and held it over them both. Rebecca rested her hand on the butt of her gun.

A salty breeze tugged at their hair, carrying with it the cries of seagulls wheeling overhead. The docks creaked beneath their feet, each step taking them farther from land. It was eerie to walk past these beacons of luxury and realize they were all empty. Bobbing tombstones hiding the vile acts their owners had committed, which led to their deaths.

As they reached the end of the long pier, Longmire raised a hand to two empty spots, each one taking up an entire dock on their own.

"They're both gone. I hadn't noticed. I'm sorry, Sheriff, it seems like I led you out here for nothing."

Rebecca frowned, glancing around and half expecting to see the glint of a sniper's rifle. But no gunshot echoed out. Instead, Longmire sighed and turned back to where she and Viviane were still standing within the gauntlet of yachts.

"Do you keep a record of boat traffic? Anything that might tell us where they went?"

Longmire shook his head but pointed to a buoy in the distance. "No logbook, but since our last conversation, I've installed cameras to monitor the comings and goings of every boat."

"Good thinking." Viviane gave Longmire an approving nod, and he managed to pull up a smile in response.

"Let's go back to my office. I can show you the footage there."

They followed him back into the marina building, where he pulled up the security footage on a computer. Rebecca leaned in closer, studying the grainy images as they revealed the truth of the boats' movements.

The *Blue Liberty* had left three days prior, its motorboat in a dry dock of sorts along the back of the marina. Then, only yesterday, the motorboat returned briefly before leaving once more, this time towed behind the *Delilah*.

"Look there." She pointed at the screen. "That's our killer piloting the boat, isn't it?"

"Hard to make out." Viviane squinted at the figure on the screen. "But it's certainly possible."

"Thank you, Longmire." Rebecca straightened. "Can you send that to me?"

He started tapping at the keyboard. "I can. And then I'm going home. My family's more important to me than anything in this marina. You can call me if you need anything else. My phone number will be in the email."

Relieved, but still a bit wary of Longmire's change, Rebecca nodded and left. Her shoulders stayed tense until the door to the marina closed behind them.

Outside, she turned to Viviane. "Did you notice anything strange about the attached motorboat when it came back?"

Viviane frowned, squinting her eyes as she searched her memory. "I'm not sure. Why?"

They climbed into the cruiser, and Rebecca pulled her seat belt on.

"The *Blue Liberty* left three days ago, right?" Rebecca began, picking up speed as she pieced together the puzzle. "That could be where the Sawyers are hiding. The motorboat returned yesterday, so they must've been getting the *Delilah* to set their trap. But when it came back, the motor was tangled with marsh grass."

She pulled out her radio and relayed the information to Lettinger, requesting a BOLO for the *Blue Liberty* and assistance in searching the nearby islands.

"While we head south to check out the marshes!" Viviane's lips curved up in a smile as she caught on.

"Exactly." Rebecca's tone was grim. The southern tip of the island, near the old vacant boathouse, was a place Rebecca knew all too well. That was where she'd first seen the body of Cassie Leigh and started her career as a law enforcement officer on this island.

26

I paced the polished wooden deck of the yacht like a caged tiger, my high heels clicking angrily. The fog thinned and swirled over the water, allowing shimmering rays of sunlight to break through and reflect off our pristine *Blue Liberty*. If the fog lifted completely, our hiding place would be exposed.

Straining my vision to the north toward the marshes surrounding Shadow Island, I once again found my fists clenched. Frustration and anger boiled within me. We'd been waiting to hear from Archer for far too long.

"Dammit." I turned, glaring at Jim and Ryker, both lounging in the luxurious seating area, doing their best to stay out of my way. "Archer should've finished this by now. We've only got one target left, and more cops keep showing up."

"We really should be leaving, dear." Jim looked over the top of his glass, inspecting the weather.

"I know. I know! But once this task is done, we'll never have to look back. Or come back." Leaning against the railing, I studied the lights in the distance, wondering if they were from fog-reflected light or an approaching boat.

"We could always work remotely." Jim's suggestion was unacceptable, and I was annoyed that he'd even brought it up. When I turned to face him, he seemed to relent a bit. "We don't need to be here when Allen's killed. You only want to be here so you can revel in it. You might have to give up this last bit of fun and settle for knowing it happened, instead of watching or listening to it."

Jim was right, but I didn't have to like it. The weather in the last few days had been a blessing. The rain and fog had allowed us to enjoy front-row seats as every obstacle to my perfect future got flattened.

A bump along the waterline rocked the boat. But I recognized the nudge. The motorboat had docked below.

Archer was back!

The hulk of a man appeared on the deck, his muscular frame dripping with sweat from his reconnaissance mission. He looked exhausted, the dark circles under his eyes betraying a sleepless night. I was disappointed he didn't bother to at least smooth his clothes before presenting himself to me.

"Finally. What took you so long? Tell me you've got Wilson's ear all wrapped up in a bow for my collection."

Archer hesitated. His voice came out strained. "It's not that simple. I've been staking out his place from a distance, but there are cops everywhere. They've got the house completely surrounded. Even his shades are drawn, so I can't snipe him from outside."

I didn't have time for his excuses. "That's your problem, Archer. You're the assassin. Figure it out."

"Look, I can still do this." Anger mixed with something I'd never heard from him—desperation?—crept into his tone. "I can break into the house, no problem. It's getting away afterward that's the issue. But if I can draw the cops away from the house, even for just a few minutes, it'll work. I just need a little time to craft a few more devices."

"Devices? What have you been doing all night?" I'd given him explicit instructions, and now it sounded like he was freelancing.

"Working on this plan." Archer gritted his teeth. "I've been trying to find a way in without alerting their security system. If I try to disable it, the company will be notified, and they'll alert the cops sitting outside."

"Then. Hurry. It. Up." I'd tolerated missteps and excuses too long. "We want to leave today." I glared at the man before me, noting his desperation to please me.

Archer nodded. "I won't let you down."

An urgent beeping pierced the stifling silence. Archer fumbled in his pocket and pulled out a small device, his eyes widening as he scanned the display.

His concern distressed me. "What the hell is that?"

"There's movement nearby." He held up the device, which looked like a tiny speaker. "They triggered the motion sensor I set up on the road to the marshes."

"Then go get rid of them!" It was beyond me why I had to connect the dots for this man. "And kill Wilson. We don't have time for this!"

Archer gave me a nod and disappeared to the lower decks.

"Good riddance," Jim muttered as Archer sped off in our boat again. He had a familiar glint in his eye, one of calculation and conniving that was so endearing. "You know...we could let your toy take out Wilson and then let the cops gun him down. Who cares if Archer lives or dies? As long as Wilson can't talk, we're in the clear."

I considered his suggestion. It was a thought I'd entertained after Archer's first failure. "If Archer somehow survives, he'll be another loose end we have to deal with."

"Should've let me buy that rocket launcher." Jim pouted, clearly bitter about the missed opportunity. "We could've blown Wilson to smithereens on our way out of the country."

"Rocket launchers on a boat?" I relished his desire to use overwhelming force, but he wasn't considering the consequences. "You really haven't thought that through, have you? Not only would it give away our location, but the Coast Guard would hunt us down in no time."

"Fine," Jim grumbled, his disappointment evident. "But if this doesn't work out, don't say I didn't try to help."

"Your 'help' is duly noted." I strained to see through the fog to the marshes for any sign of Archer's movements. Anxiety gnawed at me. After spending years controlling the world around me, fear was not a familiar emotion. But my plan, so meticulously crafted, might crumble at any moment.

Frustration and doubt clouded my thoughts like the damn fog, suffocating me and impairing my vision. I needed to picture my future. I paced as I considered how to proceed, while Jim and Ryker sat there looking too worried to blink. The tension on the yacht was palpable.

"Trust him," Jim whispered, though I knew he was trying to convince himself as well. "He'll get it done."

"Trust is the one luxury we can't afford. Not when our lives are on the line." I turned to face the two men in my life and observed Ryker's expression. I'd seen his judgmental looks before, but I was in no mood for it tonight. "What the hell are you looking at?"

He swallowed hard. "Y-you two really don't care about anyone but yourselves, do you?"

Sniveling, weak...

I took a step toward him. "Oh, spare me the melodrama. We've taken care of you your entire life. Indulged your every whim, even when you got too close to the sheriff." I fixed him with one of my deadly stares. "Don't make me regret that decision enough that I change my mind about it."

27

Murky water lapping at their shoes, Rebecca and Viviane trudged through the marshy area of Shadow Island. Yet another pair of footwear to be sacrificed for the job.

It was barely one, but the sky was a swirling gray as the fog still lingered, clinging to the briny marsh more thickly than anywhere else on the island.

The abandoned boathouse loomed ahead, its structure rotting and sinking into the swamp. Here, the air smelled strange, like a matchstick after it'd been freshly struck. It was the smell more than anything that let Rebecca know where they were.

After a psychopath had hidden within its rotting hull, the island's teenagers had been dead set on burning down the wrecked ship that was nearly as old as the lighthouse. The flames had caught, but the sodden wood fizzled out quickly. Their efforts had merely charred the rotting hull instead of eliminating it.

Knowing this area had deeper currents, where the water would suddenly be up to her hips or even shoulders, Rebecca moved slowly.

With all sounds muffled and the view limited to within arm's reach, it felt like she and Viviane were the only people on the island as they searched for signs of recent boat activity. They scanned the muddy banks, but Rebecca's mind wandered far and wide.

"Abner's death is still so surreal." Viviane's sudden words startled Rebecca.

"It's not helping any that we haven't had a moment to breathe or think since then." She darted a look at Viviane, slowing her steps. "I think Hoyt might be on the verge of retirement. It feels like everything's changing."

"I haven't heard anything about that. But then again, I've been really distracted running back and forth from the hospital to work." Viviane's dark eyes stayed focused on the waterlogged landscape. "Change isn't always a bad thing. Speaking of which, what do you think about Trent? You two have been working together a lot lately."

Rebecca considered the question, her mind shifting to Trent's recent transformation. His appearance had changed as drastically as his actions had. He even sported a scar on his cheek from a blow to the head he'd taken while acting as her backup when they'd been searching this same marsh. And though he hadn't complained about it, he had to still be recovering from the beatdown he got at the station while trying to protect Melody and the prisoners.

"He's a good deputy, but he's had a rough time lately."

"I used to think he was kind of an idiot, you know? But I can see he's trying. Greg was hard on him, but it whipped him into shape, and they seemed to bond over it." Her gaze met Rebecca's.

"Breaking bad habits is a lot harder than creating good, new ones. Greg…" Emotion threatened to clog Rebecca's throat, and she coughed to clear it. "Greg showed him the right way, and Trent eagerly soaked in all the advice."

Like walking headfirst into a darkened shipwreck when we were hunting for a crazed killer who had a tendency to attack suddenly. That had been a real rookie move.

"Trent's making steady progress," Viviane agreed. "He might never become the best deputy, but he's been through a hell of a lot. I admire how he's been working overtime, even while healing from his injuries."

Rebecca paused to stretch out the lingering pain in her back. "Plus, he realized there was a bomb on that boat before I did."

"True." Viviane dropped her gaze to the ground again. "And I'm not going to complain that he kept one of my closest friends alive."

As they continued their search, Rebecca couldn't help but agree. Trent might not have been the most competent deputy in the past, but he certainly had grit. And enough courage to turn his back on the Yacht Club, which was a lot more than most people had.

A loud sound, like a flock of birds all taking flight at once, burst from the trees behind them.

Rebecca instinctively reached for her holster, her heart pounding in her chest. "Get down."

She dropped, and Viviane followed suit a second later. They both twisted on their feet, trying to find where the noise came from. But the marshland was now silent. The only sound Rebecca could hear, besides the rapid beating of her heart, was the rustle from a soft breeze that brushed against their backs.

Seconds later, two gunshots pierced the air, dying in the thick fog before they could echo through the marshland. Without hesitation, Rebecca turned off her flashlight and signaled Viviane to do the same.

Treading lightly over damp grass, she moved away from

the deeper waters and back toward the woods and the source of the sounds.

With the way sound echoed, she wasn't even a hundred percent positive the two noises had been gunshots. Or that it hadn't been a single shot that echoed. Still, after everything that'd happened, she wasn't going to take any chances.

"Shots fired. I repeat, shots fired at our location. We need backup at the southern tip of the island, near the old boathouse." Rebecca spoke into her radio as she duck-walked forward.

"Copy that, Sheriff. Backup will be there in five minutes." Trent was smart enough to keep his voice low and soft, so it didn't carry.

Moments later, two more gunshots rang out. Adrenaline coursed through Rebecca's veins as she and Viviane pursued the shooter through the shallow wetland.

The water splashed around them, soaking their uniforms and weighing them down, but Rebecca refused to let it slow their progress. This could prove her theory that the Sawyers had been hiding out down here in one of their other boats.

Or they could simply be getting rid of the assassin they'd hired.

"Stay sharp, Darby." Rebecca kept her eyes peeled for any sign of movement or danger. "We need to find this bastard before he slips away."

The sound of a car engine caught their attention. They straightened slightly and followed the noise through the swampy terrain littered with scrubby trees and tall grasses.

As they stumbled into a clearing, Rebecca's heart sank as she saw a small black car already speeding away. The roaring engine echoed in her ears. She clenched her fists in frustration and cursed under her breath.

They strained their eyes to make out any distinguishing

features on the car, but other than its sleek silhouette, it was impossible to tell the make or model.

Her radio crackled to life in her hand, and she raised it to her lips once more, transmitting their failed pursuit. "Dispatch, we have a possible suspect fleeing the scene in a small black vehicle. We were unable to get the plate number. Issue a BOLO for the car and the area surrounding the southern marshes."

The static-filled silence was palpable as Rebecca waited for a response from the other end.

"Copy that," Elliot replied, and Rebecca knew their colleagues would leap into action.

She let out a soft sigh and returned her radio to her shoulder holster before turning to face her partner.

As they stood there, drenched and panting, Rebecca suspected things on Shadow Island were about to change drastically. For better or worse, they were all being tested by the darkness they were trying to exorcise from their town.

28

Trent Locke's back pulsed with pain in time with his heartbeat as he stared out at the wreckage-strewn waters, the wind whipping past his ears.

He, Jake, and a bunch of Lettinger's people were still processing the explosion scene, but every inch of it seemed to mock their efforts. With his training, Jake was one of the divers. He told Trent he preferred it, actually. Staying active felt better.

The divers struggled to see anything underwater. In addition to the explosion, the water was muddied by the subsequent feasting of hungry marine life, shifting tides, and hours of divers and tow boats moving around the area.

On the surface, Trent had to contend with the light rain that sent drops splattering down from the sky only to bounce back on the surface, obscuring what was happening above and below the waterline.

All while completely soaked.

Though he didn't envy his partner having to dive down and try to sort out body pieces and fight with ocean life to reclaim them, he did wish he could also wear a wet suit. At least then he wouldn't be completely soaked.

Another marker floated to the surface, and Trent hooked it with the gaff and started pulling it in. A stream of bubbles came up beside it before a diver's head, covered in a black dive suit, surfaced.

The diver swam forward, grabbed hold of the boat, and pulled off the goggles, revealing Jake's pale-blue eyes.

Trent's eyes narrowed as he saw it was yet another net full of small bits of debris. "Finding bodies and wrecked remains of a yacht isn't going to help us catch the Sawyers. Or stop them from doing this again."

The larger pieces had almost all been picked up already and loaded on the tugboats to be taken in.

Waves slapped against the side of the boat, adding to his growing frustration.

Jake glanced over at him as he took a break, hanging from the ropes draped along the boat for exactly that reason. "Maybe. Maybe not. But what else can we do? There's plenty of troopers swarming the island. And I'm not one to sit on my butt and do nothing. This is the best we can do, so we need to do it."

A cry from another of the boats drew their attention. Three divers were working together to pass over a gray corpse to the people waiting on that ship.

Trent recognized the outfit from the previous night.

As they pulled Christian Mallard's body from the water, the blank gaze in his wide-open eyes sent shivers down Trent's spine. He remembered the terror on the man's face mere moments before his death, the same man he'd promised to protect.

Guilt gnawed at him like a relentless beast, and he hated it. "Our best, huh? Seems like that's all we ever do, and it's not enough to stop these guys before they move on to their next victims."

"Sometimes, that's all we can do." Jake's words were laced with understanding. "And every person we catch is another victim who wasn't targeted or killed."

Trent sighed, knowing that the deaths of both Mallard and Wallace would haunt him forever, the same as Abner's would. He couldn't blame the other deputies for not trusting him. He'd betrayed them for years and not thought twice about it.

As the weight of his thoughts threatened to crush him, a crackle came over their radio. It was Rebecca, her voice tense.

"Shots fired. I repeat, shots fired at our location. We need backup at the southern tip of the island, near the old boathouse."

"Copy that, Sheriff." Trent reached to help Jake as he started climbing aboard. "Backup will be there in five minutes." He kept his voice low and soft so it wouldn't be overheard on Rebecca's end.

This was the break they needed. He exchanged a glance with Jake as he tumbled onto the deck and waved for him to take the wheel.

Without another word, Trent started the engine and spun the boat. They'd need to watch for any remaining debris as they made their way toward the Waterman's Memorial.

Their borrowed boat sliced through the waves as they sped down the coast of Shadow Island. The salty spray stung Trent's face. Jake stayed as low as he could while stripping the top of the dive suit off and reaching for his utility belt.

As they hit the southern shore, the fog got thicker, cloaking them in a shroud of mist that seemed to swallow them whole. The rain fell away like a distant memory, leaving only the rhythmic bobbing of the boat and the hiss of water against its hull. Trent drove the boat as close to the shore as he could, carefully navigating around hidden rocks and submerged trees. Jake stripped off the legs of his suit and dropped them next to his flippers with a squelch.

As they approached the area where Rebecca had directed them, the crashing of branches caught Trent's attention.

He slowed the boat as Jake slipped into his pants. The roar of a car engine dwarfed the sound of their own motor. A black sedan came into view, hurtling toward them as it raced off the solid land and into the reed riddled water.

It smacked the surface of the water at a high speed and then stopped, its nose tipping downward as it slowly filled with water and began to sink.

There was no driver inside.

The eerie gurgles and bubbles hung heavy over the water's surface as they both scanned the vicinity for any other signs of life or danger. The car might've been empty when it went into the water, but someone must have revved the engine first or rigged the accelerator through cruise control to get it there.

Somewhere, in the mist and trees, was the person Rebecca had been chasing. The person who'd been firing a gun.

Trent stayed hunched low over the helm while Jake knelt against the gunwale. Both focused on the sight in front of them.

"Shit." Fear was evident in Jake's voice.

The stillness was broken by a fluttering of wings overhead as a flock of seagulls flew past them with shrill cries, seeming to mirror their own mounting unease.

"Sheriff, Locke and Coffey here on the southeast shore near the tributaries. We found the car." Trent's spoke urgently. "It's sinking, but there's no driver."

"Copy that." Rebecca's tone was grim and slightly breathless. "Keep an eye out for any sign of the shooter."

"Oh, trust me, we are." Trent's heart raced as he surveyed the landscape, searching for anything that might lead them to the one responsible.

There had to be something, some clue they could latch onto. Because if there wasn't, all they'd have left were the bodies, the guilt, and the sinking feeling that they'd never catch the Sawyers.

29

Rebecca slogged through the dank swampland, her shoes sinking deeper into the sludge with each labored step. The marsh had been a breeze compared to this, yet she kept up her pace, pushing through the cloying air that stuck to her skin like wet spiderwebs. She stole a glance at Viviane beside her, the other woman's expression set in a focused look. Viviane's gaze raked across their surroundings while her coiled hair was plastered to her neck from the humidity.

"Godforsaken swamp." Viviane slapped viciously at the low hanging branches that threatened to encroach on their journey.

"Keep it down," Rebecca hissed, nervously skirting around the branches without breaking stride. "We have to find that shooter fast."

They finally reached their cruiser, which was parked on the side of a dirt road. Both women jumped inside. Rebecca got behind the wheel and turned it on, grateful for a brief break from the humid swampland. She pointed it north and then went east, following Trent's directions.

It didn't take long before they arrived at the area he'd

indicated. They were barely a mile away from where they'd stopped chasing the shooter on foot.

The black sedan she'd seen earlier was nearly submerged by this point. Only the trunk and rear wheels remained visible. Dark bubbles still rose to the surface, marking its slow descent into the murky depths.

Rebecca parked the cruiser again and climbed out, her hand resting on the butt of her gun. The shooter must've ditched the vehicle here soon after they'd started chasing him. But how the hell did he get away? And where was he now?

She scanned the sparse trees around them, looking for any sign of movement while activating her radio. "Locke, Coffey, did you see which way the driver went?"

"No, Boss," Jake responded from his radio on the boat. "We didn't see anyone at all. Only the car right before it splashed down in the water."

Rebecca turned a slow circle. "Keep an eye out for anything suspicious. We're going to search the area."

"Copy that." Locke's deep voice crackled over the radio, his usually quiet demeanor giving way to a tone of urgency.

"Yeah, Boss," Jake chimed in. "There's more boats on their way."

Rebecca and Viviane began their search, looking for any sign of where the shooter might have gone. Or where the car came from.

That first part was easy, and they were able to walk back in the direction the rear of the car pointed. It was high ground with firm soil under their feet. Packed enough to handle a vehicle driving over it.

But that only gave them a slight indication of direction and nothing else. As they waded through the swampy terrain, it became clear that finding tracks would be impossible.

After several days of rain, even the solid higher ground was completely saturated. There was an inch or two of standing muddy water on top of everything, hiding what was underneath.

There was no way to discern a visible track, no matter how hard they looked. The trees were also soaked, with branches that bent easily instead of snapping, so there was no clear path among them either.

Water covered everything. Their own tracks became instant puddles before blending in entirely.

"This is like trying to find a needle in a haystack." Viviane grunted, having to pull her shoes out of soft soil, indicating they'd gone too far from the route the car had to have taken. She started walking backward to Rebecca, her frustration evident in her labored breaths.

"Except this haystack is wet and smells like dead fish." Rebecca shared her friend's irritation. She glanced back to where they'd just come from, noticing that her view of the boat where her deputies were waiting was blocked now. The fog was thinner in the trees, but the vegetation limited their line of sight.

They continued walking in circles, searching for anything that might provide a clue. The only things that stood out were the sounds of backup rumbling in the distance as Rebecca tried to pick a path that would lead them back to where she'd first seen the car.

Somewhere along this line, the driver must have bailed. Otherwise, Jake and Trent would've seen him.

Trent's voice came over the radio again. "Sheriff, the tow truck is here and is about to pull the car out. You might want to come back and check it out."

"Will do, Locke. We're not having any luck out here, so we're on our way." She motioned to Viviane, and they hurried back to the location of the sunken car.

As they approached, Rebecca's mind raced with possibilities. What could they find to help them track down the shooter? And how much time did they have before he struck again?

Whatever we find had better be good. We can't afford more delays.

Rebecca was impressed at how close the tow truck managed to get to the car and how quickly he'd hooked up the vehicle.

But she was a bit annoyed that her deputies had separated like that until she spotted two more boats heading their way.

As she got closer, and the tow truck hoisted the black sedan out of the water, she could see that it was a Honda Accord and read the license plate number.

"Boss," Trent radioed, in lieu of yelling.

"I see it, Locke." They made eye contact for confirmation. "Viviane, grab the forensic kit from the cruiser."

"Got it." Viviane put her gun away and ran to the back of Rebecca's vehicle.

Climbing into the driver's seat, Rebecca typed in the license plate number on the onboard computer. The name Jim Sawyer flashed onto the screen as the registered owner. Rebecca felt a grim satisfaction.

The chains continued to crank and grind, reeling in the car, sending sheets of water streaming out of every seam. Pushing the computer aside, Rebecca got out to join Viviane as she waited.

With a final *slosh* and *thump*, the black Accord came to a rest. Rebecca glanced over and got a wave from the driver, letting her know it was safe to approach.

Considering she was already soaked, Rebecca stepped forward and opened the driver's door. Gallons of water rushed out, nearly knocking her feet out from under her.

Shuffling carefully, she moved out of the way to let Viviane step in with the forensic kit.

Viviane set to work collecting fingerprints from the steering wheel. Her fingers flew deftly over the surface as she made preparations.

Rebecca looked over Viviane's shoulder as she delicately pulled back the tape. She held it up and revealed a clear, usable print. Both women exchanged excited glances, knowing this could be the break they needed.

The splashing sound of approaching tires made Rebecca turn to see who was arriving. A large van, marked with *Crime Scene Response Team*, rolled to a stop.

"Perfect timing." Rebecca nudged Viviane, then pointed to the new arrival. "You might want to hand that print off to them."

"Yeah, Boss." Viviane raised her arm and flagged down one of the technicians. He came over at a jog, and she passed him the evidence. "Can you do a rush job on this? We need answers, fast."

"Sure thing," the tech replied, his eyes serious. "I can take it to the lab on the mainland right away. You should have results in no more than twelve hours, if we can find a match."

"We'd appreciate it." Rebecca nodded her thanks.

"Hey, Sheriff," Trent called over the radio, drawing her attention once more, "you might want to check the trunk."

"I'll go get the crowbar from the cruiser." Viviane started to walk off.

Rebecca raised a hand to stop her. "No need." She leaned into the still-open car door and plucked the keys from the ignition. "Let's hope we won't find any nasty surprises."

As she approached the trunk, Rebecca couldn't banish the image of her ex's lifeless gray body crammed inside. No one had seen Ryker since he'd been hauled out of his jail cell.

She shook her head forcefully, trying to dispel the horrifying thought.

"Ready?" Viviane spoke quietly, letting Rebecca know she'd caught on to her discomfort.

"I've got this." With a deep breath, Rebecca inserted the key and turned it. The trunk lid popped open with a soft click.

Instead of a body, the trunk revealed an assortment of wet gunpowder bags and several cut lengths of two-inch-wide PVC pipes. Rebecca examined them closely, dread settling in the pit of her stomach as realization dawned.

Two forensic techs who'd been approaching stopped to look, as well, one sucking in a worried breath.

"Oh hell." Viviane pressed the back of her wrist over her mouth. "What are these assholes planning now?"

"What is it?" Trent's worried voice came over the radio.

"Pipe bombs." Rebecca cleared her throat, cued her mic, and repeated herself. "The killer's used two already, but there might be more."

"Well now, that's not good." Jake's slow, drawn-out words nearly made Rebecca giggle before she tamped down the fear that birthed her sudden bout of silliness.

That was one hell of an understatement.

"Call Rhonda. Tell her to warn everyone. We might not be done dealing with explosives. And make sure the troopers guarding Allen Wilson's house also know about this."

As Viviane relayed the message, Rebecca stared at the sinister contents of the trunk, her heart heavy with the weight of their discovery. This kind of arsenal meant the stakes had been raised. They'd have to act quickly if they hoped to prevent further bloodshed.

30

Rebecca steered the cruiser through the quaint, narrow streets of Shadow Island. In the hours since they'd discovered the pipe bombs in the trunk, the sun had finally reappeared. Now it cast long, late afternoon shadows across the pavement, creating an eerie yet picturesque mood as it reflected off the soaked roads and houses. For the first time in days, she hadn't needed to use windshield wipers, and there was no fog near her.

Viviane sat in the passenger seat, scanning their surroundings for any trace of the person they heard shooting in the marsh or signs of the muscular man hired by Jim and Vera Sawyer. They could be the same person, but it could also have been Jim or even Ryker out there with them earlier, or another random hire. They'd been looking for over two hours now.

"Kinda quiet around here." Viviane broke the silence between them. "Of course, this island doesn't see much action on a Sunday in November."

"Especially not after a murder investigation's been blown

wide open," Rebecca added, her tone more serious. Glancing in her rearview mirror, she noted the continued presence of state police vehicles, indicating the staties were still processing the scene of the ditched car.

"Any word from Trent?" Viviane fiddled with the straps of her vest.

"Last I heard, he and Hoyt borrowed a motorboat to search the waters around the island. They're coordinating with the Coast Guard too. Jake is searching by the shops. We've got this place pretty much locked down." Rebecca tensed as she spotted movement, but it was only an unhappy cat tiptoeing across a drenched lawn.

As if on cue, Rebecca's phone buzzed. She pulled the device out and held it up to see an incoming call from Rhonda. She tapped the speaker button. "Rebecca here with Viviane. Any updates?"

"Good news. My CSI techs finished their rush job on the fingerprints, and we've got a match." Rhonda's excitement was evident in her voice. "His name's Kurt Archer. Lives in DC. I'll send some more information over to your computer."

"Great work, Rhonda." Rebecca's grip on the steering wheel tightened. "We'll take a look as soon as it comes through."

"Ladies, this guy appears to be a contract killer. Stay safe, you two." Rhonda ended the call.

"Kurt Archer, huh?" Viviane's brow furrowed as she said his name. "That doesn't sound like your run-of-the-mill hired gun."

Rebecca gave a small bark of laughter at the miffed tone. "It's not like only people named Shooty McShooterton can become hired killers."

"Yeah, but with a name like that, he should be on Team Good Guy and use a bow and arrow. It would be way cooler." Viviane's nose wrinkled in amusement.

Rolling her eyes, Rebecca pulled over to a quiet spot on the side of the road. "Let's see what Rhonda dug up on him."

"All right, here's what we've got." Viviane turned the computer toward Rebecca. "Kurt Archer. Quite the résumé on this guy. Nothing related to archery…" The screen flared to life as new files arrived, and Viviane began to read them out loud.

"Born and raised right outside DC, Kurt Archer was a star quarterback in high school before enlisting in the Army. He did several tours in Afghanistan as a highly decorated sniper."

"Explains the shooting skills," Rebecca muttered.

"Right? After his third tour, he moved north of DC. Got a job at a shooting range, but it only lasted a few months." Viviane paused, scrolling through the information. "He was arrested for murder in a turf dispute but released due to lack of evidence."

"Sounds like someone the Yacht Club would love to hire. And shows he's not afraid to work for criminal organizations. We already know he's not worried about directly going after the cops either."

"But wait, there's more." Viviane scrolled farther. "Three years ago, he was arrested again for possession of an explosive during a routine traffic stop. Somehow, he managed to avoid prison after the judge declared a mistrial. No mention of why, but it seems someone intervened on his behalf."

"Convenient. And has the Yacht Club's M.O. all over it." Rebecca's temples throbbed, a combination of anger and incredible disappointment at the justice system that failed people so badly. "What about now?"

"Nothing much. No employment records for the last five years, but he's living in Dupont Circle, a nice part of DC. He's clearly got income coming from somewhere." Viviane clicked through to another file, revealing a mug shot. "This is him. A dead ringer for the man seen breaking into Jay Griles's place. Tall, muscular, wide build, bald."

Rebecca studied Archer's mug shot. He fit the image of the man from their collected surveillance footage.

"Send that out to everyone. Update the BOLO." Rebecca glanced around, taking in the serene island landscape. "We've got a killer to catch, and he's most likely on the island or nearby."

"Sending now." Viviane's fingers danced across the keyboard.

"We need to find this guy, and fast."

"Agreed." Viviane closed the file. "He's our best lead so far, and if he's here on the island, we need to bring him in before he disappears into the vastness of the mainland."

"All right, let's keep moving." Rebecca put the SUV into gear and merged back onto the road.

As they continued their search, she wondered how Archer was getting around the island unnoticed. It was like he was a ghost, blending in with the shadows. The mix of storms and fog certainly could be helping with that. This weather was making everyone's jobs so much harder than they needed to be.

"Keep your ears out too," Rebecca warned. "We still don't know the reason for the shooting back in the marsh. He could be shooting wildly. If that was even him." She bit her lip, not saying it could be Ryker on the run from his own parents. Viviane didn't need to be reminded that they also needed to keep an eye out for the man who'd escaped from their jail.

"Understood." Even as she spoke, Viviane's dark eyes continued their vigilant scan of the streets. "We'll find him. He can't hide forever."

She was right. The Yacht Club had been smothering

Shadow Island like a poison gas for too long. Rebecca wasn't going to let Kurt Archer slip through their fingers now.

But where in the hell was he?

Rebecca steered her cruiser past quaint shops and idyllic homes that suddenly seemed cloaked in secrets.

31

Restlessly moving like a storm within a teacup, I stalked the cabin on the lowest deck of my superyacht. Worry plagued me as I continued to stalk my confines. Could I trust Ryker that his confession was phony?

I'd been on edge ever since Archer had departed to deal with whoever had triggered his motion sensor. A loud commotion had erupted shortly after, including gunshots that echoed through the blanketing fog.

I'd turned to the only person in the world who I could truly trust, imploring Jim to take the jet ski and investigate. But neither Jim nor Archer had returned, leaving me alone with my dark thoughts. And Ryker. Whoever was out there, I hoped Archer had distracted them with those gunshots.

The alternative was unthinkable. Surely, both of them hadn't gone off and gotten themselves caught. Or killed.

At the sound of something cutting through the water, I rushed to peer out the side of the yacht. Jim was approaching on the jet ski but keeping it slow. The engine had been specially modified to run quieter, and when it was coasting, it was nearly silent. Relief washed over me as I ran to help him stow it.

"What happened?" I glanced toward the marsh.

Jim wiped sweat from his brow. "I kept my distance, hiding behind some trees. It looks like Archer ditched my car in the water as a distraction. I'm not sure what he has planned, but they're hauling my car out now." His eyes narrowed. "But Archer wasn't there."

"Dammit." I pulled out my phone and dialed Archer's number.

When he picked up, all he said was, "Don't worry. I'll take care of this." Then he hung up. He hung up! The fool. If he managed to accomplish his task, I'd still need to discipline him to correct his insubordination.

"How are we supposed to not worry when we're practically on top of a police investigation?" I glared at Jim, hoping he had a plan. "We should just leave. Take the boat and go. We've got money. Even if Allen Wilson testifies, we could buy a lawyer who could get us out of this mess. We've made sure there's no physical evidence to tie us to anything. Or we could find somewhere abroad to relocate, change our names."

Jim shook his head. "No, you were right earlier, my love. We need to finish this here and now. We've given Archer one last chance to end this. Then we can leave with no loose ends and no reason to look over our shoulders for the rest of our lives."

My heart was pounding as I weighed Jim's words. He was right, of course, yet my instincts were screaming that we needed to flee. The mental image of our Accord being hauled from the water, while the sheriff and her deputies swarmed all over it searching for evidence to use against us, taunted me.

I relented. "Fine, one last chance."

The consequences of what would happen if we didn't manage to get away clean haunted me as I stood on the deck, shoulder to shoulder with my partner in crime. Whispers of betrayal seemed to hang in the air. But there was no turning back now. We'd see this through to the bitter end, no matter what it took.

There was no question, no hesitation, that I'd do whatever was necessary to ensure our survival. I'd leave everything behind if I had to. Jim leaned into me, and I chanced a glance at Ryker, slouched in a chair, looking utterly pathetic. His presence was a constant source of disappointment and frustration.

Despite my disgust with him, it was possible my wayward son could offer a fresh perspective on our predicament. "Ryker." Unsurprisingly, I startled him. Always best to keep him off balance. "Do you have any opinions on the matter?"

He glanced up, his eyes empty of any fight or passion, and merely shrugged. How could he not care? This was his fate too. He betrayed us when Luka was sent to kill the sheriff, but then he'd righted his wrong by providing a false confession. I wasn't sure where his loyalties lay, but I was repulsed that he didn't sense the urgency of the situation.

This pitiful creature had emerged from my own loins. I should've aborted him when I'd had the chance. Or cut the cord that tethered his little toy boat to our yacht when the grown-ups were having our fun and he'd been in our way.

"Tell me, how did we end up with a son like you?" I regarded him with the same contempt I had for the club members who were now fish food. "After all your training. Everything we did for you. Your father's daughter has bigger balls."

"Sorry for not growing up to be a sociopath, Mother." Sarcasm laced his words. "How inconsiderate of me. I know you tried. Hey, I got your eyes, if it's any consolation."

My hands tightened into fists, and I considered pummeling him right there. Although I saw no trace of my strength in Ryker, I couldn't kill my own son. But there were other ways to ensure his silence.

"Just because I said I would let you live doesn't mean you're guaranteed to keep your tongue, hands, or eyes."

Ryker paled, his pretty eyes widening in fear. "I'm sorry, Mother. I meant no disrespect. I'm so worried about you and Father, it's making me short-tempered. You don't need to maim me. I can still be useful."

I snorted. "How?"

He swallowed hard. "I know this sheriff. I gave you copies of the reports showing what she did on that island. You know from reading them that she doesn't back down. She killed a lot of men by herself." He took a deep breath. "Now she's coming after us."

I silenced him with a glare and turned away. Yes, Rebecca West had finished killing the cartel men. But Ryker gave her too much credit. After all, she'd had all her deputies with her for much of the battle. Five men winning against fifteen was respectable, but it wasn't the miracle Ryker thought it was. His pretty lady had help when she'd taken down those fifteen men.

My phone buzzed. It was Archer, and his voice was steady, confident. "Everything is in position, Vera."

Relief washed over me, and I exhaled a breath I hated myself for holding. "How soon can you get here so we can all leave?" I was more than capable of taking out my own garbage, but having a trained killer by my side had a few advantages.

"It won't be long now. I'm using that dead idiot's car. Coach Brighton. The spineless guy who you told me abused the boys on his team." There was a hint of dark amusement in his voice. "I took his car key the night we busted Ryker out. Kept it nearby just in case, since I knew offing him was always part of your plan. I'm a pro, and I plan for all outcomes. I'll call back once everything else is ready."

His resourcefulness and premeditation were admirable. I side-eyed Ryker, still sitting there like a useless lump, and I was grateful to have someone as capable as Archer on my side.

"Good. We'll be waiting for you."

My tension began to unravel, and I allowed myself a small smile. We'd been given a lifeline, one last chance to put an end to this nightmare and escape. Nothing would stand in my way now. Freedom was close, and I intended to seize it, no matter the cost.

The darkening marshes surrounded us. Even the usually calming water lapping against the hull failed to offer me comfort. I gripped my phone tightly as I waited for Archer's next words.

"Get ready to go." His voice was a low growl. "I'm coming in just a few minutes. After I kill Wilson, I'll steal his boat and come back to the yacht ASAP. Then we can run away together. Make sure you're ready for me."

My lips curved into a predatory smile. "I've been ready for hours." I purred the words into the phone, motivating him to success with his own lust. "Hurry, so I can show you how happy it will make me to know this is all over."

Jim stood nearby, his arms folded across his broad chest. Our eyes met, and he offered a knowing smirk in return, fully aware of what I'd implied.

"Understood." Archer's eagerness was unmistakable.

Ending the call, I slipped my phone into my pocket and took a deep breath, trying to tamp down my desires and steady my racing pulse. The time had finally come to sever the last remaining thread that threatened to unravel our carefully constructed lives.

With renewed hope, my thoughts became clearer, and I began to scheme. "Jim, get everything ready. We're leaving as soon as Archer returns."

He nodded and moved to stow the remaining items that littered the deck. His efficiency and dedication were admirable. It was a stark contrast to Ryker, who sulked by the railing, his face contorted with fear and resentment.

I addressed my deviant child much as I would a servant. "We're leaving soon. I suggest you make yourself useful for once."

His eyes flicked up, the tawny swirl of his irises reflecting the turmoil within him. He hesitated for a moment, but I glared at him.

Finally, his training must've kicked in, because his shoulders wilted. He knew he had no options other than what I gave him.

As his mother and trainer, it was a lesson I'd taught him over and over throughout his mediocre life. A familiar progression of thoughts would trail across his face, starting with defiance and ending with resignation. But he'd never talk back to me.

"Fine."

I couldn't afford to dwell on his evident reluctance. There was work to be done.

With preparations for our imminent departure underway, I allowed myself a few precious moments to envision the future—one without fear, without suspicion, and most importantly, without Allen Wilson or Rebecca West. A shiver of anticipation ran down my spine. We were going to get out of this and start over.

"Soon, this will all be behind us, and we can retire into the life we deserve."

32

Salty air stung Trent's cheeks as he and Hoyt skimmed along the coast of Shadow Island in the motorboat that he and Jake had used earlier. They'd dropped Jake on shore to search for their suspect in town. The sun had only recently set, and a bank of fog and clouds merged with the water, casting an eerie calm over the scene.

Trent peered through a pair of night vision binoculars into the distance, searching for any signs of the tall, muscular man they believed was responsible for driving Jim Sawyer's Honda Accord into the ocean and for various other, bigger crimes.

"Can't figure out why someone would drive their car into the ocean like that." Trent rubbed his eyes with a salt-covered finger and regretted it immediately. "It doesn't make sense."

"Maybe it's meant to throw us off. Make us think he's dead. Or that he's hiding evidence, which could be true. Heck, maybe those explosives were supposed to go off. We won't know anything until forensics is done with it." Hoyt steered the boat closer to shore. "Keep us busy while he does something else."

Trent blinked, trying to clear his eyes. It would be his ass on the line if he missed something on land. Maybe no one else would blame him outright, but he would blame himself.

Rebecca's voice crackled through the radio. "We have the fingerprint results from the car in the water. I'm sending that match to all of you now."

"That was fast. We need to get one of those handheld scanners ourselves, Boss." Hoyt was grinning as he responded to the sheriff.

Rebecca's snort sounded even worse through the radio. "Sure. I'll get right on that. After we rebuild the station with all the copious money in our budget. Oh, wait, new gear and a remodel of the station ate most of that."

"That remodel was barely done. You think we can get Larry to fix everything on warranty?"

Trent gaped at Hoyt.

Hoyt shrugged it off. "If we can't laugh at life, we might as well lie down and die."

That sounded a bit defeatist and totally unlike the deputy Trent had worked with for so long. Before he could respond, however, Rebecca beat him to it.

"That's what insurance is for. And Larry's dealing with enough shit right now. Don't forget, Ryker had full access to everything Larry worked on. Including all those new security cameras that went up."

Hearing that, Trent flinched. News of Ryker's jailbreak had already spread through town. A lot of people were worried about their own safety now, after having trusted the man with spare keys to their rentals and homes. He'd been a reliable handyman.

His phone buzzed, and Trent pulled it out of his pocket. It was a text from Rebecca, not words but a mug shot of a menacing figure with a shaved head and piercing eyes. *Kurt*

Archer. We've finally got a name and face for the man terrorizing the island.

Trent felt a mix of hope and frustration. They knew who they were after, but the man seemed to have vanished into thin air. He showed the image to Hoyt.

As they coasted up to the dock where they had initially picked up the boat, Hoyt stared at the edge of town visible behind it. "You know, the Bean Tree Coffeehouse isn't far from here."

For a moment, Trent wondered if the older man was randomly letting him know where they were. But Hoyt continued, a half smile on his face.

"You look beat, Trent. How about we grab some coffee before we continue?"

Trent started to refuse, but Hoyt cut him off. "After everything you've gone through the last couple of days, we need to keep your health up. Can't have you getting dehydrated or hungry. My treat."

Surprised by the uncharacteristic offer, Trent was touched. He tried not to let his happiness show. "A hot cup of coffee would be nice about now."

He had to grab the gunwale as Hoyt suddenly turned the boat to the dock. "And a bear claw. We need to keep our sugar up, too, after all. Even cops get to take breaks."

Trent coughed to hide a laugh as Hoyt expertly maneuvered the boat up against the dock.

With quick movements, they tied off the boat and hopped onto the worn wood. Trent had to nearly jog to keep up with Hoyt as he made a beeline to the cruiser they'd left parked there.

As Trent slid into the passenger's seat and buckled in, a low growl greeted him. He grinned but didn't say a word about Hoyt's complaining stomach as the other man put the cruiser in gear and headed for town.

Bean Tree Coffeehouse beckoned with its warm lighting and inviting atmosphere. The aroma of yeast and sugar greeted the men as they entered, momentarily pushing aside the weight of their investigation. Hoyt approached the counter rubbing his hands together like some kind of Bond villain. "A black coffee and a bear claw, please."

Trent was going to simply ask for a coffee when his stomach growled even louder than Hoyt's had in the cruiser.

Hoyt raised an eyebrow and gestured to the young girl behind the cashier. "And go ahead and add whatever else this hungry guy wants as well." He smirked, motioning toward Trent.

That small act made him feel more like part of the team than anything else had. Warmth spread through him, and he stepped up to the register. "I'll take a hazelnut latte and a chocolate croissant. Please."

She nodded and took Hoyt's card. "You can go ahead and get your pastries while I make your drinks."

Trent turned to the display case and grabbed both their orders, passing over Hoyt's before taking a giant bite of his. Since it was near closing time and the place was deserted, Trent was surprised there were any bear claws left.

Hoyt gazed around the cozy shop, a wistful expression crossing his face. "Wallace loved this place. He always said their coffee was 'the good stuff.'"

An unexpected surge of regret hit Trent, and he blurted out. "I'm sorry, Hoyt. For everything. For Wallace. For being such a shitty deputy. For running off at the mouth. For Abner." Heat ran up his neck to his cheeks, and he prayed the blush wasn't visible. "I feel like I don't deserve this position."

Hoyt lifted his hat, running a hand through his hair.

Trent was certain he'd screwed up. Word-vomiting like that in public—even if the cashier couldn't hear them over the high-pitched hiss of the milk being steamed—was proof.

Jeez, why did he suddenly feel like a kid on the first day of school again?

"Abner's death wasn't your fault, and Boss said you saved her life. I trust her judgment." Hoyt paused, meeting Trent's gaze. "Maybe you shouldn't be so hard on yourself."

Before Trent could respond, the barista leaned over the counter and handed them their coffees. She hesitated, frozen in place. And then she glanced over her shoulder at a young man wearing an apron in the back of the store. He waved her on in an encouraging manner.

Trent lowered the cup, waiting for her to bring up whatever was bothering her and her coworker.

She finally spit it out in a rush. "I found something strange in the alley behind the building. It's like a weird pipe thing. It's just lying on the ground."

Hoyt and Trent exchanged glances. Trent recalled the pipes Rebecca had found in the trunk of the car belonging to Jim Sawyer. Maybe Archer or Jim had been trying to hide something from them. "Wait here. We'll take a look."

"It's out back. You can walk through." She reached over to the hinged section of the counter and lifted it. "It's to the left of the door."

Trent stepped through the gap in the counter and headed through the kitchen. The coworker who'd goaded the barista waited near the back exit. Before walking through it, Trent looked over his shoulder.

Hoyt was in the kitchen, motioning both baristas toward the front of the shop.

Trent ducked his head out the door and looked to the left.

The white PVC pipe was easy enough to spot lying on the dark ground. Both ends were capped. A black band ran around the middle, probably electrical tape. Under that band was a small square of black plastic. A wire ran from that square and disappeared into one capped end.

Trent stepped back and pulled the heavy door to the coffee shop closed.

The employees seemed more at ease as he calmly walked back to join them. Which was reassuring, since his gut was a churning mess. "Is anyone else working tonight?"

"Only the manager. He's in the office."

Hoyt's head twitched, and Trent nodded.

"Get him and get out. Evacuate the building. Go straight out the front, across the street, and keep your head down. We need to investigate this."

The two employees ran off, the girl heading for the office while the boy ran the other way, calling over his shoulder. "I'll check the bathrooms."

"We'll do that. You three get out of here." Hoyt dropped his voice. "What is it?"

"It looks like a pipe bomb. Two-inch diameter. About a foot and a half long. Any clue how big of a blast something like that would make?" Trent walked beside him as they left the kitchen and started to clear the building.

"No idea." Hoyt shoved the bathroom door open. It was a single seater, and no one was hiding in it. He pointed to the door.

Trent grabbed his cup from the counter as he passed it on his way to the door. With the other hand, he grabbed his radio from his shoulder. "Sheriff, we've got a pipe bomb at the Bean Tree Coffeehouse."

"I'm sorry, Deputy. Can you repeat that? I thought you said a pipe bomb."

"Yes, ma'am, I did." He pushed through the front door and caught Hoyt staring at the cup in his hand. Trent scowled and glared at the cup that was in Hoyt's hand, indicating his hypocrisy.

The three employees were already across the road, watching them. Hoyt gestured at them to stay where they were, then headed left as Trent went right. They needed to evacuate the nearby businesses as well.

Rebecca's voice finally came back after a long, silent stretch. "Make sure everyone's out of the area. Bomb squad is on the way. They're still close because they've been helping to sort the pieces from the boat explosion and checking the bomb parts found in the Accord that was pulled out of the water."

Before Trent could respond, a deafening explosion sounded in the distance. He dropped and spun around, then stared in confusion when he spotted the coffeehouse still standing.

That didn't come from the pipe bomb? Then what...?

Another explosion ripped through the air. This one from the opposite direction of the first one.

What the hell is going on here? Trent started running across the street. "There's more than one bomb!"

As his foot hit the opposite curb, the bomb behind Bean Tree Coffeehouse detonated, sending him tumbling.

33

Rebecca gripped the steering wheel, her knuckles white as she and Viviane sped along the coastal road. Eerie shadows danced through the fog and reflected off the churning sea. A series of explosions echoed through the air, rattling the cruiser windows and reverberating through their chests.

"Jesus," Viviane muttered, her dark eyes wide as she peered out the windshield. "What's going on?"

"Stay focused." Rebecca's pulse pounded in her ears as she pulled over on the side of the road. They were halfway back to town, still surrounded by trees and homes. Before she went racing in, she wanted to know where they were heading and what they were heading into. She radioed the other deputies, voice tense but steady. "Check in. Are you all okay?"

One by one, Trent, Jake, and finally Hoyt responded.

"No one here is hurt. We managed to evacuate the building and the only one next to it that had anyone in it. But Locke spilled his latte when the bomb behind the coffeehouse went off."

Rebecca ignored the crack, knowing laughter was Hoyt's

favorite way to deal with work stress. "Can you tell where the last explosion was?"

"No. The last two came too close together. My ears are still ringing, and I was ass over teakettle at the time. Didn't spill my coffee, though."

Beside her, Viviane pressed a hand over her mouth to stifle her laugh.

"Look around. See what you can learn and report back."

"Yeah, Boss. There's a fire that started in the alley. Coffey's back there with the cruiser's fire extinguisher. Once he's done, or the firefighters show up, we'll start asking around."

Rebecca switched from her radio to her phone and called Rhonda.

"We're fine here, Rebecca. Every officer is accounted for and safe. They're already heading out to help civilians and get any injured to safety." Rhonda sounded like she was running, her words rapid and breathy.

"You've sent off every single one of your team?"

"Almost." A car door slammed, and Rhonda's voice changed as the onboard system connected in her cruiser. "I left one trooper with Wilson."

"Where did the bombs go off?" Rebecca had a sinking feeling.

"According to my people who were out looking for Archer and the Sawyers, we're certain about Bean Tree, Oyster Bay, Sand Dollar Park, and Atticus Beach. Those are the four we're sure of, but there might be more. I've got extra units on the way. And we're calling in sniffer dogs too."

"What about Allen Wilson's neighborhood?"

There was a pause. "No word on that yet."

That seemed odd to Rebecca. That many explosions and none of them went off in the areas where cops were gathered? The attacks seemed random, but Rebecca's intuition told her otherwise.

As she connected the dots in her mind of the places that had been targeted, her heart skipped a beat.

If she plotted those spots on a map, they would form a square, starting from where she last saw Archer and ending near her old neighborhood.

"Darby, I need you to listen carefully." She took a deep breath, trying to steady herself. "Call every one of the other deputies. Tell them to head for Allen Wilson's house." Rebecca yanked the wheel, spinning the SUV around.

"What's going on?" Viviane braced herself against the dash as she turned on the lights and siren.

"Those random bombs? They feel like a distraction." Rebecca's mind raced, adrenaline coursing through her veins. "I think Archer's trying to draw us away from Wilson so he can finish him off."

"Shit." Viviane relayed the orders to the others. Trent had rushed to meet up with Hoyt and they confirmed they were en route, traveling by boat.

As they raced toward Wilson's house, Rebecca felt torn. The crimson glow of flames rose in the distance, where Jake was fighting the fire at Bean Tree. She couldn't tell where the other one was coming from, though.

With the size of the pipe she'd seen in Jim's trunk, those bombs could've taken down buildings. What if there were more? If a bomb went off inside a building at the same time the others went off, Rhonda and her team might not have noticed it yet.

Especially if all the people inside can't call for help or let people know they're hurt.

The idea of people trapped, injured, and screaming in panic filled her mind. She'd seen the damage that could be done to the old brick buildings that made up so much of the town. The image of Luka Reynold crushed under the rubble was going to stick with her. That horrific image could be replaying all over their island.

She wanted to stay and help. To search every building and make sure no one was left behind. But in her logical mind, she knew that the key to stopping this madness lay at Allen Wilson's doorstep. He was the last loose end for Vera and Jim to eliminate. Much as she wanted to help the civilians, she needed to leave that to the first responders.

The wail of several different sirens sliced through the air as Rebecca and Viviane sped out of town. "We need to get to Wilson's house. Rhonda's people are already working the bomb scenes. If I'm right, this is Archer's work. We have to stop him before he takes out Wilson and we lose our last witness against the Yacht Club." She had to say the words out loud, not only to comfort Viviane, but to soothe her own screaming conscience.

"God, what if you're wrong?" Viviane whispered, her voice cracking under the weight of the guilt threatening to consume her. "What if we should be helping these people instead?"

"Viviane, listen to me." Rebecca took another steadying breath. "I know it's hard, but if we can stop whoever's doing this, then all these people will be safe. The state police, ambulance, and firefighters are already heading there. Trust me."

"Okay, I trust you." The steel was back in her voice. "But, Rebecca, please…let's make sure this bastard pays."

"Count on it."

As they entered Wilson's neighborhood, the absence of state troopers stood out to Rebecca immediately. The once-peaceful street now seemed ominous, and she knew they were walking into the lion's den.

"Boss." Viviane nearly choked on the word. "Look."

Parked in front of Wilson's house, the lone state trooper car stood sentinel, its red-and-blue lights unlit, the driver's side door hanging open. Sprawled on the ground was Trooper Dolph Burke. He hadn't been on duty earlier when she'd been here.

Hell, how he'd been cleared after killing a surrendering suspect was beyond her. Rhonda had opened up an internal investigation to investigate the investigator who'd cleared Burke for duty. Though Rebecca remembered a couple of his trooper friends vouching for him on-scene.

All those investigations are over now.

The top of his head was missing. Clearly, Vera and Jim weren't just eliminating Yacht Club members. It seemed anyone who'd ever worked for them was meeting an early demise.

"Dammit." Rebecca slammed on the brakes, skidding to a stop. She fought the bile rising in her throat. As she stared at what was left of Burke, relief, guilt, and anger warred within her.

"Over there." Viviane nodded toward a brand-new Chevrolet Camaro LT parked in Wilson's yard. Deep ruts in the grass led to the area it was parked. "That wasn't there before."

"No, it wasn't. And look." Rebecca indicated Allen Wilson's front door. It was standing wide open.

She called in to relay news of Burke's death, which let Hoyt and Trent know what was happening as they rushed to the scene in the motorboat. She recited the Camaro's plate number and disconnected.

"You think that's Archer's car? Maybe he waited for the other troopers to leave, then came here for his real target…or targets." The openly corrupt Burke was more than likely on the list of associates the Sawyers might've wanted to eliminate.

"Then let's not waste any more time." Viviane's voice shook with fury. "Let's find this son of a bitch and make him pay for what he's done to our town."

Backup was on the way, but Viviane was right. There was no time to waste.

Rebecca pulled her gun as she jumped out and ran for the house.

34

Allen Wilson's pulse pounded in his skull as he cowered behind the sofa in his living room. The sound of bombs exploding in the distance still echoed in his ears, a cruel reminder that he should've heeded the sheriff's warning and left Shadow Island when he had the chance.

The cop who'd been inside with him ran out as another explosion went off down the street. Crawling toward the window, he peeked through a crack in the curtains. "Dammit all. I should've listened. Why didn't I take her offer?"

He watched Coach Brighton's car race toward his house before sliding to a halt in his front yard. Allen tried to steady his breath. And it worked...until he saw the Grim Reaper get out and approach his house, guns in both fists.

The trooper who was leaning in his open car door while he held his radio had turned to face the commotion. But before he could do anything else, a series of gunshots rang out, and the trooper, weapon drawn and firing back, dropped out of sight.

"Jesus Christ!" Allen gasped, his eyes wide with terror.

In a panic, he scrambled from behind the couch, ran up the

stairs, and rushed into his bedroom, slamming the door shut behind him. With trembling hands, he shoved the heavy oak dresser against the door, barricading himself inside. He prayed that it would be enough to keep Vera's executioner at bay.

As Allen pressed his ear against the door, he heard footsteps downstairs, accompanied by the sound of objects being thrown about. Archer was hunting him down. Each step seemed louder than the last, sending shivers down Allen's spine as the man drew closer. He knew he couldn't stay hidden in his bedroom forever.

Allen looked around as if he had never seen the room. He needed another way out before Archer made it to the second floor. Why did he run upstairs? Why hadn't he gone out the back door instead? His gaze alighted on every object around him.

Everything was either soft, delicate, or lightweight. Nothing that would make a good weapon.

Why don't I have a gun? Stupid.

Allen held his breath, fully expecting his life to be snuffed out in an instant. But then a woman's voice, shouting from outside the house, caught his attention.

"Kurt Archer! Come out with your hands up!"

Holy shit. She actually came back to save me...

Allen was covered in goose bumps as relief flooded his system and tears sprang up in his eyes. He dared to peek out from behind the bed. The dresser still stood in its place, ready to block any shooter who came running up the stairs. At least, temporarily.

Creeping as quietly as he could, Allen made his way to the window, which looked out on the front lawn.

The sheriff's cruiser was parked at the curb, not far from where the cop lay dead by his vehicle. The new lady deputy was standing near the front walkway. As Allen went up on his toes and leaned against the glass, he could see Sheriff West standing to the side of the front door, gun in hand. She and her deputy were so intent on watching the door, they didn't see him in the window.

A few seconds later, another deputy drove in and parked near the sheriff's SUV. Turning from the window on shaking legs, Allen approached the blockade he'd made at the door. He pushed the dresser to the side. He had to be ready to run as soon as the sheriff told him to. This time, he would listen. If he had to, he could take his boat. He'd pocketed his keys earlier, just in case.

Holding his hand flat against the door, he twisted the knob, flinching as the catch gave, even though it was soundless. He was able to open the door the rest of the way under the cover of West's voice, once again demanding Archer come out with his hands up.

He approached the stairs, hoping for a clear path to the door.

Kurt Archer stood at the bottom of the stairs with guns in both hands as he faced the front door, his back to Allen.

Allen froze.

The sheriff and her men are going to run in to save me, and he's going to kill them.

His heart sank. His rescuers were walking into certain death if he didn't do something.

The adrenaline that coursed through his veins was a sharp electric shock, jolting him to action. He knew he had only one chance to change the course of fate that lay before them all. Summoning every ounce of courage he possessed, Allen crept halfway down the stairs, one step at a time.

Then, with a surge of uncommon bravado, he dove down the remaining steps, aiming for the man who'd come to kill him.

He felt as though he were flying, suspended for an instant in the air before gravity insisted on having its way.

His target started to turn toward him.

This is it. This is how I'm going to die.

With a thud, he slammed into the muscular man, knocking him off balance. They both went down, but Allen landed on top. The keys to his boat skidded across the floor until the small life preserver keychain dragged them to a halt by the door.

"Dammit!" Archer snarled as his guns skittered across the hardwood. "I'm going to kill you, you stupid fucker."

Allen scrambled to his feet and lunged for the door, desperate to escape the man he'd tackled. The door was only a few feet away. Surely, he could make it before Kurt retrieved his guns.

Unless Archer had yet another weapon. Which would really, really suck.

This was the worst day to give up coke.

The moment he burst out of the house, he found himself face-to-face with the familiar, stoic features of the sheriff.

Relief swept through him as the deputy ran from his cruiser and grabbed ahold of him, swinging him away from the open doorway and pressing him against the side of his house.

"Easy there." Coffey, according to his nametag, held Allen up as his knees gave out. "We're going to get you somewhere safe."

Allen gasped, allowing the deputy to lead him away from the chaos unfolding inside his home.

As they hurried across his torn-up lawn, the sound of gunfire erupted behind them, signaling the start of a fierce firefight between Sheriff West, her deputy, and Archer.

"Did we get him?" Allen's pulse was pounding in his ears.

"Can't say yet." Coffey was scanning their surroundings as

they jogged. "But we've got a team of deputies on the scene. We'll bring him down."

"Should've listened to the sheriff earlier." Allen's thoughts were a whirlwind of regret and gratitude. "I might not be in this mess if I had."

"Hey, no time for regrets now," Coffey reassured him, a hint of humor in his voice. "You're still here, and that's what counts."

It was a sobering thought, but one that ignited a newfound appreciation for life and the people who'd risked theirs to save his. With every step away from the sound of gunfire and the smell of gunpowder, he clung to the hope that he'd live to see another sunrise.

"Right." Allen gave a shaky laugh, trying to dismiss the weight of his choices. For the first time in a long time, it seemed he'd made the right one. "Still here, somehow."

"Sometimes, that's all you can ask for." A knowing smile played at the edges of Coffey's lips.

35

The acrid scent of gunpowder filled the air as Archer fired at Rebecca and Viviane. Allen had been secured and hauled off.

Rebecca didn't hesitate to return fire, her instincts kicking in like a well-oiled machine. Three shots, then duck back around the corner. Viviane was using the same tactic from the other side of the opening. She managed to do so barely in time to avoid the hail of bullets coming her way.

Archer was definitely firing two guns, since his rounds never seemed to pause.

Rebecca's adrenaline surged through her veins, sharpening her senses. The sound of breaking glass reached her ears, and she immediately knew what it meant. Rushing toward the source of the noise, she spotted Archer halfway through the back window, shards of glass surrounding him.

"Darby! With me!" Rebecca didn't spare a glance to see if the rookie deputy was following. She took off at a run outside and around to the back of the house.

As she did, Rebecca saw Coffey sitting in the cruiser with Allen Wilson beside him. The man looked terrified, his eyes wide with fear. The sight of him safe, for the moment at least, provided a small measure of relief.

"Coffey, get him to the state police station in Coastal Ridge," Rebecca said through the radio, her voice tense. "Don't let anyone but Rhonda near him until I get back."

Jake confirmed, revving the engine before peeling away from the scene, tires screeching against the wet pavement.

When Rebecca and Viviane reached the backyard, they realized how quickly Archer had moved. He was already down the dock and climbing into a motorboat. Rebecca recognized it from the list of Yacht Club member assets they'd catalogued. She watched as he fumbled with the controls before the boat roared to life, propelling him away from the shoreline.

"Dammit! Where the hell did he get the keys?" Rebecca couldn't chase him on the water. Her frustration grew with every second that ticked by, feeling helpless as Archer escaped.

But then, as if things were finally starting to turn in her favor, Hoyt and Trent's boat appeared in the distance. The sight of her fellow officers gave Rebecca a surge of renewed hope.

"Frost! Locke!" she shouted, waving them over and running to the edge of the dock. "Archer's getting away in that boat."

As the two deputies pulled their vessel alongside the dock, Rebecca hopped in. As Trent hauled Viviane aboard, she had a flinty look in her eyes.

"Locke, call this in and let them know we're pursuing Archer and to send more boats."

"Yeah, Boss. On it."

Hoyt pushed the throttle forward as they began to give chase. The boat's engine roared, slicing through the water as they pursued their quarry. Trent had to hold on tight to the railing as he raised his radio to his lips.

All the while, Rebecca thought about how this was the same way Greg had died, chasing after a suspect, vulnerable to gunfire. She prayed their bulletproof vests wouldn't fail them as it had failed the deputy.

As they raced through the waterways, they closed the distance between them and Archer's boat. The man was nothing if not resourceful, forcing them into a high-speed chase. But Rebecca was determined. She wouldn't let him slip through their fingers again.

Soon, Archer's boat flickered back into view, weaving through the numerous waterways that led out to the open ocean. The wind whipped around them, tugging at Rebecca's hair and stinging her face.

"Trent! Viviane! Get ready to return fire," she shouted over the roar of the engines. "Take him down!"

"Roger that!" Trent replied, positioning himself at the bow, while Viviane took up a spot at the stern, her eyes narrowed in concentration.

As they continued their high-speed pursuit, Archer began firing wildly in their direction. Bullets tore through the air around them, splashing into the water or pinging off the hull of their boat. Rebecca's mind raced back to Greg. She swallowed hard, pushing away the encroaching grief and guilt as her team returned fire.

The chase carried them out into the open ocean, where waves foamed white against the sides of their boats. The rougher water made their shots miss their intended target.

Not far in the distance was a thick band of rising fog.

Shit.

Archer's vessel bobbed and swayed, and Rebecca couldn't be sure if any of their shots had hit their mark. But something seemed off. He appeared to struggle with the controls, his movements erratic.

"Keep on him!" Rebecca barked, her voice hoarse from the wind and salt spray. "He can't keep this up for long!"

"Damn right." Viviane fired another round in Archer's direction.

Suddenly, Archer veered sharply to port, disappearing into the thick fog that still clung to the marshes. Rebecca's heart sank. After the incident with the Lovecraft-obsessed maniac, the last place she wanted to head into was the marshes.

"Frost, follow him in!" she ordered, desperation amplifying her words.

"Are you sure, Boss?" Hoyt hesitated, glancing back at her with concern etched across his face. "That fog is thicker than pea soup."

"We have to try." She scanned the hazy horizon. "I'll take responsibility for whatever happens. Just get us in there!"

"All right," Hoyt conceded, turning the boat toward the fog-shrouded marshes. "Hold on tight, everyone."

As they entered the dense mist, visibility dropped to near zero. The world around them faded away, leaving only the sound of the engines and the waves lapping against the hull.

36

My heart pounded as Kurt Archer pulled up alongside our yacht. The sun had dipped below the horizon, casting darkness over the marshes at the southern tip of Shadow Island. Instead of docking the boat as I'd expected, he leaped onto the deck with a catlike agility that belied his muscular frame.

"Jim! We need to go now!" Archer's panicked voice was urgent.

I looked between the two men, trying to make sense of what was happening.

"All right, all right." Jim moved toward the stairs to the helm, but Archer grabbed his arm, stopping him in his tracks.

"No, not the yacht, the speedboat." Archer's eyes darted about as if he expected an imminent ambush. "We're being pursued. The tank's been refueled, right?"

"Who's pursuing us?" Confusion, fear, and anger all fought for control of me. In all my years, I'd never seen a professional assassin this rattled. "And yes, Ryker topped off the tanks."

"Deputies," he spat out, his jaw clenched. "Now move!"

As we scrambled toward the speedboat, I spied the boat Archer had left floating free. It wasn't the one he'd borrowed from us. Dread churned in my stomach. "Is Wilson dead?" I hated that my voice was shaky, showing weakness.

"Put a bullet through his head," Archer replied without hesitation, his face hard and emotionless. "Now let's get out of here."

There was no time now for further questions. We clambered onto the larger speedboat with its full tank of gas as the sound of another vessel approached. The silhouette of an approaching boat with a handful of people broke through the fog.

My idiot "professional" had led the enemy right to us. "Son of a bitch!"

Archer opened fire on the incoming law enforcement. Bullets whizzed by, and I ducked for cover alongside Jim and Ryker in the cramped confines of the speedboat.

"Go!" Archer shouted while continuing his covering fire. The engine roared to life as my skilled husband maneuvered the boat away from the yacht.

I fell forward as it suddenly stopped.

"Dammit! What now?" Adrenaline stabbed at me like a knife.

"Stay down." Archer shouted as bullets sailed all around us.

I turned toward Jim to find Ryker in the captain's seat. Jim was on the floor of the boat where Ryker had apparently shoved him, scrabbling to get up. At the most critical moment, Ryker was defying me.

My son is a traitor.

"Ryker, get moving! You're going to get us all killed!"

"Better us than them." His defiance rang clear in my ears. "You treat me worse than a dog. Dad treats me worse than the kids and women he sells on the black market. They at least always got water."

"Dammit, Ryker!" The boy was stubborn, I'd give him that. Of all the traits he could've gotten from me.

"Enough of this." Archer pulled two guns and trained them on my son.

My heart lodged in my throat, but before Archer could fire, Ryker launched himself at the man, knocking the weapons from his hands.

They grappled, fists flying, but Ryker was losing ground. The once-obedient hired gun seemed hellbent on going rogue and punishing my son.

"Leave him alone, Archer!" I commanded, trying to regain control of the man. "Focus on the damned cops! Jim, drive the boat!"

Archer paused, panting. Just before I thought I'd have to reprimand him again, he turned and leveled his gun at the bitch sheriff who was closing the gap between our boats.

Jim gunned it away from the chaos, and I was glad for this much faster vessel.

Ryker stood straight up, maneuvering himself in front of Archer.

My blood ran cold as his intentions became clear. "Ryker, get out of the way! You're blocking Archer's shot. Move!"

"No. This has to stop!" He pulled his shoulders back, looking directly at me in a way he seldom did. "Mother, I lied before. Rebecca knows everything. My recorded confession was very detailed. You and Father will spend the rest of your lives in prison."

Just when I'd thought he was redeemable, he showed his true colors.

"You're a pathetic failure," Archer sneered as he inserted a new clip into his gun. "You should've listened to Mommy." Raising the weapon, he pulled the trigger.

The world swirled around me as red blossomed across Ryker's chest.

My poor, pathetic little boy stumbled back, his eyes wide with shock and pain.

Jim dove from the captain's seat and lunged at our son. I watched helplessly as Jim's fingers grasped at Ryker's shirt as he tumbled backward.

But it was too late.

"Nooooo!" The word was like razors coming from my throat.

Ryker's body hit the water, disappearing beneath the dark waves.

"Damn you, Archer!" Jim cursed, getting the boat back on track. The speedboat surged forward, leaving Ryker behind.

"You killed my son." I stared at Archer, filled with rage and grief. "You killed my boy."

"Vera, I had—"

"No!" I raised my hand to silence him. Like the little bitch he was, Archer stopped talking. "Give me your gun. I'll finish this business myself." I extended my hand, daring him to defy me.

I hadn't expected him to comply, but he did, handing over the weapon with a look of confusion and remorse. Like a scolded child, Archer meekly waited for my next move. I had no intention of keeping him waiting.

"Thank you. It's nice to have someone who listens to my orders."

Archer began to smile despite the gunfire trained on us.

With one practiced motion, I aimed the gun at Archer's chest and fired. Blood spattered my face, but I didn't blink.

His eyes widened, betrayed and perplexed, as I reached out to him. "Need a hand?" Before he could reply, I pushed him overboard so he could join Ryker's corpse in the sea.

Archer's body sank beneath the water, and I smiled bitterly, knowing that justice had been served.

"My love." Jim looked back at me. "What do we do now?"

"Survive." My determination had never been so strong. "That's what we've always done, and that's what we'll keep doing. We still have your girl."

Jim sighed but nodded. "Gemma's a good girl. The same way her mother was."

The engines roared as my husband propelled us forward. But I could only look back. "Goodbye, son."

He'd been a whopping nine pounds and ten ounces when he came screaming into the world, with a head full of dark hair and lungs that could have blown down any house.

He'd been so precious. Learning to crawl, then toddle, then run. I'd had such high hopes for him as his muscles filled out and his dick had grown long and thick. Such a man I'd borne. So perfect in every way.

On the outside.

His insides, though, didn't have what it took to take over the empire I'd created. When had I known he was soft where it mattered most?

Sixteen? Earlier?

But, deep inside, I'd never given up hope that he'd change.

A bullet whizzed by my ear, forcing me back to the present. Filled with rage and sorrow, I fired blindly back as the speedboat raced away from the scene, leaving only the sound of waves and sirens in its wake.

37

Rebecca's heart pounded as she and her deputies raced through the lifting fog, guns firing. Four figures were crammed onto a speedboat. Archer was wrestling with a younger man.

Her heart stopped, and she halted fire as she recognized Ryker, standing up like a target with a bull's-eye on his back.

He's alive.

But why was he fighting Archer?

Before she could connect the dots, the fighting stopped. A single shot rang out, and Ryker fell backward.

As if in slow motion, Rebecca screamed as Jim Sawyer lunged for his son. But he wasn't fast enough, and Ryker's body hit the water.

"Noooo!" Rebecca's cry met and danced with the same cry as Ryker's mother.

As Rebecca stood frozen, Hoyt tried to close the gap between the two vessels. Trent and Viviane stopped firing but kept their guns up and aimed.

Another shot rang out, and Archer stumbled. Rebecca

watched in horror as Vera Sawyer pushed her hired assassin over the edge of the boat.

Hoyt maneuvered the boat toward the bodies.

Between the boats, two shapes started to resolve in the water as they got closer. Kurt Archer's large form floated several yards from Ryker's. Her former boyfriend's tawny eyes were wide open, seeing nothing.

"Ryker!" Rebecca shrieked, straining her throat. Despite everything he'd done to her, she never wished this on him. He'd tried to protect her in the end. Maybe she hadn't been so wrong about him…

Rebecca dropped down, leaning over the gunwale, desperate to reach him. But she couldn't. Instead, she turned, her voice filled with urgency. "Trent, help me get him out! He's going to freeze in the water if he's seriously wounded."

Trent nodded and stretched an arm out. He managed to wrap his fingers in Ryker's shirt and yank.

As he pulled Ryker closer, the extent of the damage done by the hollow-point bullet became clear to everyone in the boat. Rippling water spouted up from the center of Ryker's chest.

Rebecca's mind refused to accept what she was seeing. *How can water act like that? Shooting up like…*

The massive, gaping hole in the middle of Ryker's chest finally registered. The sight sent a chill down Rebecca's spine, and her stomach clenched in shock and grief.

"Jesus," Viviane whispered from beside Rebecca, her dark eyes wide with horror.

"Ryker's gone, Rebecca." Hoyt was gentle but firm, his own face a mask of pain.

Trent's arm relaxed, releasing the man's corpse back into the water, hiding the wound. "We'll come back for him. Right now, we need to stop the Sawyers."

Rebecca swallowed hard, nodding at Hoyt.

He gunned it.

Blinking back tears, she forced herself to focus on the task at hand. Ryker was dead. There was nothing she could do for him any longer. "Catch up to those murderous bastards. We're not going to let them get away with this."

As they pursued the Sawyers' speedboat, Jim drove recklessly while Vera fired shots at them. Rebecca gripped her gun tightly, trying not to think about Ryker's lifeless eyes. A familiar mixture of rage and sorrow was trying to engulf her, but she pushed it down, focusing on her aim.

"Come on, Rebecca!" Trent shouted over the wind. "We can't let them get away!"

Rebecca gritted her teeth and raised her weapon, taking careful aim that she timed with the bouncing of the boat.

Finally, a bullet struck Vera's shoulder. She slumped over, clutching the wound. The speedboat slowed, Jim distracted by his injured wife.

Vera tried raising her gun and firing again. But her aim was wild and off target, giving Rebecca and her deputies an opportunity to close the gap. After only a few shots, Vera collapsed.

Rebecca's heart pounded furiously in her chest as the gap between them and the Sawyers shrank. She adjusted her grip on her weapon, keeping it steady against her sweaty palms. She exchanged a quick glance with Trent, whose eyes were blazing with an unspoken promise. They would not fail.

"Get ready!" she shouted, bracing herself as Hoyt expertly steered them alongside the Sawyers' boat.

As the sides of the boats ground against each other, Vera managed to pull herself up using one of the seats that ringed the back of the vessel.

Rebecca leaped onto their deck.

Trent followed suit, launching himself at Jim. The force of the impact sent both men crashing into the steering wheel, causing the boat to spin out of control for a few terrifying moments.

Rebecca toppled backward but flung out a hand, catching hold of Vera's bloody jacket and pulling her off balance. Vera's gun went flying.

"Dammit! Let go of me!" Vera bit Rebecca's arm. Hard.

Rebecca punched Vera in response, forcing the woman to release the viselike grip on her flesh. "Stay down!" she growled.

Blood coated the older woman's teeth as she spat obscenities.

As Rebecca pinned her to the boat's deck, she noticed a tiny gap in Vera's lower row. Glancing at the bite imprint on her arm, she couldn't help but smirk. Bailey had found this bite pattern on Mary Bergman's body weeks ago.

"Looks like we'll be adding child sex offender as well as psychotic bitch to the list of your charges." Rebecca flipped the woman over, straddling her. "Your cellmates are going to love you."

"And the fish are going to love the little chunks of your body I toss out to them," Vera spat. "You never should have come to my island. It's because of you that my son is dead!" Her face contorted with rage as she fought to get up, her movements wild and desperate.

"You're—"

The boat rocked violently in the water, throwing Rebecca off balance. She fell back hard, her head slamming into something that caused stars to burst in her vision.

Trent and Jim were still grappling at the helm, with Trent gaining control, but Vera used the wave to scramble away from Rebecca. She stumbled toward the other edge of the boat, blood dripping from her gunshot shoulder like a crimson waterfall.

"Look what you've done!" she screamed, waving

frantically at Shadow Island in the distance. Vera grabbed her gun by her feet, her eyes wild with pain and hatred. "You've taken everything from me! My business, my family, my whole world!"

"Damn right I did." Rebecca managed to rise to her feet. "Someone needed to. And it's about time you faced the consequences."

They both raised their weapons.

Rebecca knew only one of them would make it out alive. Time seemed to slow, and Rebecca thought once more of Ryker.

He had his mother's eyes.

"I'll see you in Hell," Vera whispered.

They fired in unison, the explosion of the shots echoing across the ocean to the edge of the horizon.

38

Hoyt stood at the edge of the grave, his eyes red-rimmed and bleary. Beside him, Viviane's swollen eyes glistened with unshed tears. Both wore their dress uniforms, black bands wrapped around their badges in mourning. Across from them, Jake maintained a stoic expression, regret etched onto his face, while Trent appeared haggard, the weight of loss bearing down on him.

Rhonda, head bowed in prayer, also wore the somber black band around her badge. The citizens of Shadow Island had come out in droves to pay their respects to the man who'd devoted so much to keeping their island safe. It was a touching scene, filled with pain while showcasing the dedication of every member of the Shadow Island Sheriff's Office.

Rebecca scanned the unfamiliar faces in the crowd and realized these were Greg's friends—the ones he'd turned to when he needed help. Men and women who'd assisted her repeatedly without ever needing recognition. As she blotted her eyes with an already damp tissue, Rebecca thought about how long Greg Abner had been a part of this community. They would all miss him deeply.

"Abner would've appreciated this turnout," Hoyt murmured, his voice thick with emotion.

Viviane nodded, swallowing hard. "He was always there for us, wasn't he?"

"Every time," Hoyt agreed, his gaze drifting over the gathered crowd.

"Greg's fishing buddies from back in the day." Viviane had noticed Rebecca's curiosity. "He saved more than a few of them from trouble over the years."

"Seems like he touched everyone's lives." Rebecca could not keep her voice from wavering.

Nor could she help but reflect on her own survival in the face of recent events. Had it not been for her Kevlar vest, Rebecca wouldn't be standing here today. Vera had managed to fire a shot, which landed center mass.

She had a bruise and some soreness, but nothing more.

Rebecca's own aim had been true in that crucial moment. And as a former FBI agent and the current sheriff of Shadow Island, she'd helped bring justice to this small town.

"Greg was one of a kind." Melody's face was blotchy from crying. "I don't think we'll ever find someone like him again."

"His spirit will live on through all of us," Rebecca assured her, placing a comforting hand on Melody's shoulder.

"Excuse me, ma'am," Jake chimed in, his eyes meeting Rebecca's gaze. "I just wanted to say thank you. Greg would've been proud of how you handled everything."

"Thank you, Jake. We all did what needed to be done." Rebecca was not entirely successful in maintaining her composure.

Trent approached, his dark eyes filled with pain. "You know, Abner taught me most of what I know. He was tough on me, and it made me a better deputy."

Rebecca gave him a sad smile. "He believed in you, Trent. And he'd be proud of you too."

She knew his legacy would live on in the hearts and minds of those he'd left behind. Despite the destruction and chaos that had recently plagued their island, they would rebuild and move forward, united by the memory of a man who'd dedicated his life to keeping them safe.

The sun peeked through the clouds as the mourners moved from Spring Street Church to the beach. A gentle breeze carried the scent of seaweed, saltwater, and charred buildings, adding to the lingering mood of sorrow. Rebecca took a deep breath, filling her lungs with the crisp ocean air. It was a small comfort, a reminder that life would go on despite the recent tragedies.

Huddled together by the water's edge, the deputies began sharing their memories of Greg Abner. Waves lapped at the shore like an attentive audience, gently embracing the sand before receding once more.

"Greg made me feel welcome from the start." Rebecca managed a faint smile through her tears. "He insisted on calling me 'ma'am,' even after I told him it wasn't necessary. It was his way of showing respect, and that meant a lot to me as the new sheriff."

Hoyt nodded, his eyes distant but warm. "Also as a way to make up for that radio conversation we had that you weren't supposed to overhear."

Rebecca broke out in laughter, remembering when she'd first gotten her radio and caught Greg and Hoyt gossiping about her like a bunch of old men at a church social.

She'd barely even met Greg at that point, and all he'd known about her was from Trent's angry rantings. They were rehashing all the decisions she'd made so far, most of which they didn't approve of.

Needless to say, everyone had come a long way since then.

"Greg also had a true passion for fishing, you know? He spent every spare moment out on the water. But he didn't hesitate to come out of retirement to help mentor Trent." Hoyt gave Trent's shoulder a warm squeeze. "He was devoted to the people of this island until the end."

Trent shifted uncomfortably, his gaze fixed on the horizon. "Greg…was a hell of a trainer. He didn't sugarcoat things, and he pushed me to be better. I owe a lot to him." His voice wavered, betraying his emotions.

"You know, Trent," Hoyt continued, "Greg spoke highly of you. He saw your potential, and he was proud of the progress you've made. We all are."

Tears welled up in Trent's eyes, and he quickly brushed them away. "Thanks, Hoyt. That means a lot."

As they continued to reminisce, Rebecca found herself reflecting on the events of the past few days. The island had been ravaged by the Yacht Club's reign of terror, leaving scars that would take time to heal. Buildings were in ruin, lives had been lost, and their once-peaceful home now bore the weight of grief.

But there was hope too. Allen Wilson was safely off the island, set to testify against the criminal organization that had caused so much suffering. And Jim Sawyer, the only other survivor of the Yacht Club, would pay for his crimes.

Rebecca was certain it was his initials that had been burned into Elaina Roth's body. At last, the evil that had plagued Shadow Island was eradicated.

39

Rebecca leaned against her cruiser, the cool metal pressing against her back, as she watched her station get rebuilt. Things were looking up on Shadow Island. A few days after the shootout with the Sawyers, Meg Darby had woken from her coma. Doctors had run batteries of tests and found no lasting effects from either attempt on her life.

Everyone had been relieved by this positive outcome. Viviane spent much more time by her mother's hospital bed now that she was awake. Of course, in true Meg fashion, she hated all the fuss that was surrounding her. On more than one occasion, she'd told Rebecca she was eager to begin her work as the Chair of the Select Board. She felt as though she'd already "wasted" too much time.

She'd been devastated by the news of Greg Abner's death. He'd been a deputy the whole time Meg had worked the dispatch desk. And now he was gone, another friend lost in the line of duty. Another hole in her life that would never be filled.

Jim Sawyer hadn't said much once he was in custody, but he did confirm that Trooper Burke had been on their payroll and had been eliminated when they realized he was one of the troopers tasked with guarding Allen Wilson.

The recorded statements from Reynold and Ryker would ensure Jim Sawyer never walked free again. Rebecca was grateful that they'd been careful to follow procedure so a high-powered defense attorney wouldn't be able to get Sawyer off on a technicality.

In the wake of all the destruction, Rhonda Lettinger had offered some good news. Gemma Roth, Jim Sawyer's illegitimate daughter, had donated the vast majority of her inheritance from Elaina Roth to a charity serving troubled youth. Apparently, the mysterious daughter loved the theater and had taken the remaining portion of the life insurance payout and donated it to nonprofit community theaters in the region.

The girl understandably desired a new life and wanted to rid herself of any ties to her birth parents, especially since Jim was still alive. She'd recently turned eighteen, and with a little help from Rhonda, was starting over with a new identity, unencumbered by a history she'd had no control over. Gemma's story was remarkable and stood in contrast to the path Ryker had chosen.

Rebecca sighed audibly as she watched the construction crew hustling in front of the sheriff's station, their movements accompanied by the cacophony of nail guns and power tools. A fine film of dust hung in the air, mingling with the mildly singed scent of freshly sawed wood. It had been a long and difficult two weeks, but Shadow Island was rebuilding.

"Can't wait to have that new station," she said to herself, observing as the crew finished the frame of a wall. This wasn't the only crew working like this, but most buildings hadn't suffered serious damage from the pipe bombs like her station had, and there were no other fatalities from them.

Forensics figured out the bombs were hastily made, intended as a distraction so Archer could kill Allen Wilson.

The reporters wouldn't leave them alone. Everyone wanted to know what happened here. A criminal conspiracy, a series of mysterious explosions on a vacation island—top-shelf news. Fortunately, they were starting to lose interest, but not entirely.

"Excuse me, Sheriff?" A reporter approached her, notebook and pen in hand. "I've heard you used to work for the FBI. Why did you leave? Did it have something to do with the criminal organization you just took down?"

Rebecca sighed again. *Crap.* This could get a lot hairier. She'd hoped they wouldn't dig into her background. It was the last thing she needed.

"Look, I left the FBI for personal reasons." Her tone was curt, and she avoided eye contact. "And no, it didn't have anything to do with any criminal organization."

"Are you sure?" The reporter pressed on, sensing her discomfort. "You're not hiding anything, are you?"

Rebecca clenched her jaw. Of course they would try to connect her past to the present chaos. Despite her urge to snap at the reporter, she forced a smile.

"Listen," she said, trying to maintain an air of authority. "I came to Shadow Island because I wanted a fresh start. I assure you, my past has no bearing on what's happening here."

The reporter scrutinized her for a moment and then scribbled something in his notebook. Rebecca reminded herself that he was only doing his job.

"And just a few more questions, if you don't mind." He smiled at her as if certain she wouldn't mind.

The problem was, a few questions always led to a few more questions. Then a few more after that. She opened her mouth, prepared to give him a quote that no editor in their right mind would print in their newspaper, when her phone buzzed.

She pulled it from her pocket. Elliot's name showed on her screen, and she frowned. He was covering dispatch from his house until they could get the station rebuilt.

She turned and answered her phone as she walked away from the nosy reporter. "What's going on?"

"Sorry to interrupt, Sheriff. But I got a call about a body of a teenage girl found at the cemetery."

"Dammit." The word slipped out before she could stop it. She pinched the bridge of her nose, willing herself not to lose her cool while the reporter was still lurking. "Is she buried?"

"No, that's the thing. She's just…lying there."

"All right, I'm on my way." Rebecca hung up and got in her cruiser.

As she sped toward the cemetery, she thought about the challenges Shadow Island had thrown her way since she'd arrived. Nothing ever seemed to go smoothly here. But she was determined that the fresh start she sought when she arrived was still possible. And she'd make sure that Shadow Island became a safe haven for all who craved serenity.

The End
To Be Continued...

Thank you for reading.
All of the Shadow Island books can be found on Amazon.

ACKNOWLEDGMENTS

How does one adequately express gratitude to all those who have transformed a shared dream into a stunning reality? Let us attempt to do just that.

First and foremost, our families deserve our deepest thanks. Their unwavering support and encouragement have been our bedrock, allowing us the time and energy to translate our collective imagination into the words that fill these pages. Their belief in our vision has been a constant source of strength and inspiration.

As coauthors, our journey has been uniquely collaborative and rewarding. Now, with Mary also embracing the additional role of publisher, our adventure has taken on an exciting new dimension. This transition from solely writing to also publishing has been both a challenge and a joy, opening doors to share our work more directly with you, our readers.

We are immensely grateful to the entire team at Mary Stone Publishing — a group who believed in our potential from the very beginning. Their commitment extends beyond editing our words; it encompasses the tireless efforts of designers, marketers, and support staff, all dedicated to bringing our stories to life. Their expertise, creativity, and passion have been vital in capturing the essence of our tales and sharing them with the world.

However, our greatest appreciation is reserved for you, our beloved readers. You took a chance on our book, generously sharing your most precious asset—your time. It is our fervent hope that the pages of this book have rewarded that generosity, offering you a journey worth taking and memories that linger.

With all our love and heartfelt appreciation,

Mary & Lori

ABOUT THE AUTHOR

Nestled in the serene Blue Ridge Mountains of East Tennessee, Mary Stone crafts her stories surrounded by the natural beauty that inspires her. What was once a home filled with the lively energy of her sons has now become a peaceful writer's retreat, shared with cherished pets and the vivid characters of her imagination.

As her sons grew and welcomed wonderful daughters-in-law into the family, Mary's life entered a quieter phase, rich with opportunities for deep creative focus. In this tranquil environment, she weaves tales of courage, resilience, and intrigue, each story a testament to her evolving journey as a writer.

From childhood fears of shadowy figures under the bed to a profound understanding of humanity's real-life villains, Mary's style has been shaped by the realization that the most complex antagonists often hide in plain sight. Her writing is characterized by strong, multifaceted heroines who defy traditional roles, standing as equals among their peers in a world of suspense and danger.

Mary's career has blossomed from being a solitary author to establishing her own publishing house—a significant milestone that marks her growth in the literary world. This expansion is not just a personal achievement but a reflection of her commitment to bring thrilling and thought-provoking stories to a wider audience. As an author and publisher, Mary continues to challenge the conventions of the thriller genre, inviting readers into gripping tales filled with serial killers, astute FBI agents, and intrepid heroines who confront peril with unflinching bravery.

Each new story from Mary's pen—or her publishing house—is a pledge to captivate, thrill, and inspire, continuing the legacy of the imaginative little girl who once found wonder and mystery in the shadows.

Discover more about Mary Stone on her website.
www.authormarystone.com

Lori Rhodes

As a tiny girl, from the moment Lori Rhodes first dipped her toe into the surf on a barrier island of Virginia, she was in love. When she grew up and learned all the deep, dark secrets and horrible acts people could commit against each other, she couldn't stop the stories from coming out of the other end of her pen. Somehow, her magical island and the darkness got mixed together and ended up in her first novel. Now, she spends her days making sure the guests at her beach rental cottages are happy, and her nights dreaming up the characters who love her island as much as she does.

Connect with Mary online

facebook.com/authormarystone

x.com/MaryStoneAuthor

goodreads.com/AuthorMaryStone

bookbub.com/profile/3378576590

pinterest.com/MaryStoneAuthor

instagram.com/marystoneauthor

tiktok.com/@authormarystone

Made in United States
North Haven, CT
28 April 2024

51865122R10139